A Nancy Drew
Christmas

Nancy Drew

DIARIES™

A Nancy Drew Christmas

CAROLYN KEENE

Aladdin

NEW YORK LONDON TORONTO SYDNEY NEW DELHI

This book is a work of fiction. Any references to historical events, real people, or real places are used fictitiously. Other names, characters, places, and events are products of the author's imagination, and any resemblance to actual events or places or persons, living or dead, is entirely coincidental.

ALADDIN
An imprint of Simon & Schuster Children's Publishing Division
1230 Avenue of the Americas, New York, New York 10020
First Aladdin paperback edition October 2020
Text copyright © 2018 by Simon & Schuster, Inc.
Cover illustration copyright © 2018 by Erin McGuire
Also available in an Aladdin hardcover edition.
All rights reserved, including the right of reproduction in whole or in part in any form.
ALADDIN and related logo are registered trademarks of Simon & Schuster, Inc.
NANCY DREW, NANCY DREW DIARIES, and related logo are
trademarks of Simon & Schuster, Inc.
For information about special discounts for bulk purchases, please contact
Simon & Schuster Special Sales at 1-866-506-1949 or business@simonandschuster.com.
The Simon & Schuster Speakers Bureau can bring authors to your live event.
For more information or to book an event contact the Simon & Schuster Speakers Bureau
at 1-866-248-3049 or visit our website at www.simonspeakers.com.
Series designed by Karin Paprocki
Cover designed by Nina Simoneaux
Interior designed by Mike Rosamilia
The text of this book was set in Adobe Caslon Pro.
Manufactured in the United States of America 0820 OFF
2 4 6 8 10 9 7 5 3 1
The Library of Congress has cataloged the hardcover edition as follows:
Names: Keene, Carolyn, author.
Title: A Nancy Drew Christmas / by Carolyn Keene.
Description: First Aladdin hardcover edition. | New York : Aladdin, 2018. |
Series: Nancy Drew diaries ; #18 | Summary: Trapped in a beautiful Montana ski resort
with someone bent on destruction, can sleuth Nancy Drew, wearing a leg cast,
solve the crime in time to save the holiday season?
Identifiers: LCCN 2018019435 (print) | LCCN 2018025880 (eBook) |
ISBN 9781534431652 (eBook) | ISBN 9781534431645 (hardcover)
Subjects: | CYAC: Mystery and detective stories. | Skis and skiing—Fiction. | Resorts—Fiction. |
Christmas—Fiction. | BISAC: JUVENILE FICTION / Mysteries & Detective Stories. | JUVENILE
FICTION / Holidays & Celebrations / Christmas & Advent.
Classification: LCC PZ7.K23 (eBook) | LCC PZ7.K23 Fb 2018 (print) | DDC [Fic]—dc23
LC record available at https://lccn.loc.gov/2018019435
ISBN 9781534431638 (pbk)

Contents

Dear Diary,

WHAT WENT WRONG?

I should really know by now that no vacation of mine will go smoothly. But a ski disaster that lands me in a giant cast and a wheelchair just hours into the trip? Now that has to be some sort of record.

And the disasters have not stopped with my mountain wipeout. There's been a sabotaged opening dinner and mysterious hotel room break-ins, and now a couple of rival detectives are sneaking around the resort. No one knows if these events are linked, or who could be behind any of them. What's worse, I keep running into dead ends, and Christmas is only days away. Can I solve this case before Santa comes to town? Or will this Montana resort be ruined before New Year's?

CHAPTER ONE

~

Going for the Gold

THE DREADED DOUBLE BLACK DIAMOND. The most dangerous trail on the mountain. Most skiers take one look down the impossibly steep slope and ski the other way. Not me. I'd been training for this my whole life.

Cold wind smacked me in the face, a steady sheet of falling snow shooting past me like I was a Nancy Drew–shaped rocket ship skiing through space at warp speed. My skis carved up the pristine slope, white powder flying as I slalomed through a gauntlet of densely packed pine trees that would have taken out a lesser athlete. I was in the zone. Out in front of my skis. So balanced my skies slid over moguls like performance tires over freshly paved road. The kind of perfect run skiers dream about.

"Yes!" I wanted to shout, but the most dangerous part of the run was coming up. *Keep your focus, Nancy,* I thought. If I was even a few inches off when I hit the last rocky drop-off, they'd be carrying me out on a stretcher.

I shot toward the ledge, visualizing the airborne flip that would propel me over the fifteen-foot drop to the crowd waiting below at the finish line. But maybe one flip wasn't enough. . . . I was going to go for two!

And then I went airborne, flying through the . . .

DING, DING, DING . . .

"Please return to your seats and fasten your seat belts as we prepare for our final descent into Border View Regional Airport," the flight attendant announced over the plane's loudspeaker, snapping me awake.

"Huh?" I mumbled, rubbing my eyes and looking around at the other passengers.

I was airborne, all right. It just wasn't on a double black diamond ski slope. It was on a plane!

I chuckled, laughing at my ridiculous dream. I'm really good at solving mysteries. Skiing, not so much.

But that was about to change!

I looked out the window at the snow-covered peaks stretching across the landscape thirty thousand feet below, where I hoped to make the leap from wobbly beginner to unshakable expert. Okay, I'd probably settle for decently balanced intermediate. A girl can only learn so much in a week!

That's how long I was going to be staying at the Grand Sky Lodge, the newly renovated eco-friendly ski resort perched right on the Montana-Wyoming border.

My dad's law firm had represented the lodge's co-owner, Archie Leach, on a real estate development case a few months back, and I'd done a little sleuthing to dig up the evidence my dad needed to win the case. Detecting has always been a hobby of mine (my best friends, George and Bess, might swap the word "hobby" for "obsession"), and sometimes it comes with cool perks. Archie had sent a giant fruit basket to thank us, which was pretty nice of him. The nicest thing about it wasn't the fruit, though. It was the invitation that came with the basket for an all-expenses-paid trip to the Grand Sky Lodge's grand reopening the week before Christmas!

"Word is Leach and Alexander Properties put a lot of moolah into revamping this place," the stylish woman in the seat next to me observed as she flipped through the Grand Sky's brochure. "They're touting it as *the* model for environmentally sustainable ski resorts. They talk as much about wilderness conservation, renewable energy, carbon footprints, and locally sourced goods as they do the skiing. We'll see if it's the real deal or a publicity stunt to cash in on the eco craze."

My dad and I weren't the only ones who'd gotten a special invitation to the lodge's grand opening. I don't know if theirs came with a fruit basket, but the popular travel magazine *Travel Bug* got one too. The writer they sent, Carol Fremont, turned out to be my new seatmate after my dad had to reschedule his flight for a last-minute deposition on one of his big cases.

Carol gave the Grand Sky Lodge's recycled-paper brochure a skeptical flick with a well-manicured fingernail.

"Archie Leach really does believe in sustainability," I told him. "I haven't met his business partner, Grant Alexander, but I know from the work my dad did for their firm that Archie plans to make it the focus of all their new development projects."

"Well, if it's all as grand and green as they claim, then it'll make a killer feature for the magazine," Carol replied. "The eco trend grabs eyeballs too, and I'm hoping to land the cover story for print *and* online."

"I think sustainable businesses are a lot more than just a trend," I told her. "If enough businesses get on board, it could make a huge difference in the fight against climate change. I think it's great that a travel site with as many readers as *Travel Bug* is raising awareness by featuring places like Grand Sky Lodge."

"As long as it's my name people see on the byline, I'm all for it," she quipped.

I was starting to get the impression that Miss Fremont wasn't the most objective journalist. I just hoped for Archie's sake that she gave the Grand Sky a great review.

"What I'm really excited about is their new restaurant, Mountain to Table," I admitted, my mouth watering just thinking about it. "I've been dying to try Kim Crockett's food since she swept *Top Chop Challenge*. It's one of my favorite shows."

"It's another great angle for the story, that's for sure," Carol said. "You don't see many celebrity chefs leaving fancy big-city restaurants to run a kitchen in middle-of-nowhere Montana. The farm-to-table movement may be hot with foodies in the city, but trying to turn a remote mountain into a fine dining destination, now *that's* a challenge. . . . Hey, maybe I can get two feature stories out of this!"

She flipped open her laptop and started typing a note to herself.

"Excuse me, ma'am," the flight attendant chirped, leaning over Carol's seat. "You'll have to close that until we land. We'll be on the ground in just a few."

Carol wasn't much of a conversationalist after that. She started typing furiously into her phone instead, and as soon as we landed, she stalked off to baggage claim, talking to herself, dictating notes into her earbuds.

Not that she had very far to walk. The airport wasn't exactly an international hub. In fact, it was downright tiny.

With Dad still back in River Heights, I was traveling solo for now. I didn't mind, but I usually had Bess and George with me on trips like this, so it felt little strange being on my own. I couldn't wait to get to the lodge and tell them all about it.

One thing seemed clear the second I stepped into baggage claim. I might have been the only person in the whole airport without their own ski gear! The baggage belts were full of it. Ski bags must have outnumbered suitcases two to one. Grand Sky wasn't the only ski resort around—there were a handful within a few hours' drive on either side of the Montana-Wyoming border. And apparently, just about everyone at the airport was headed for one of them.

I'd just caught sight of my bag and was on my way to grab it, thinking I'd soon be a good enough skier to warrant a set of my own skis too, when . . .

"Oomph!" I blurted, as I tripped over a ski bag I hadn't noticed and tumbled headfirst toward a terrified-looking little girl!

I was inches away from plowing into the poor kid when a powerful arm grabbed me around the waist and lifted me back onto my feet.

"Oh gosh, I'm so sorry," I apologized to my rescuer, and turned around in embarrassment, expecting to see one of the macho ski dudes who'd been waiting for their gear.

"No problem," said an athletic twentysomething woman an inch or two shorter than me. "Sorry about the obstacle course."

With the sun-bleached blond streaks in her dark

hair and stylish Burton-brand gear, she looked like she could have stepped out of a ski magazine. But with the action-hero strength she'd exhibited catching me mid-fall, she could have sidelined as a superhero. I could see a long, thick scar peeking out under the cuff of her tapered fleece pants as she kicked the ski bag I'd tripped over back toward the pile of gear.

She grinned at the little girl, who was still frozen in place, and ruffled her curly hair. "We're going to have to work on those reflexes, kiddo. We're teaching you how to ski, not how to be a tree."

The girl nervously bit her lip.

I smiled at her. "Well, I managed to wipe on out on skis without even leaving the airport, so you'll probably be a better skier than me in no time!"

The girl blushed and hid behind the woman, who gave me a wink.

"Okay, guys, gather your gear," she announced to another girl and a boy who had been goofing around by the baggage carousel. "The Grand Sky Lodge is supposed to have a van waiting for us outside."

"Hey, it looks like we're headed to the same place!" I said, offering the woman my hand. "I'm Nancy."

"Liz," she said with a smile and a death-grip handshake as she nodded to the kids. None of them looked older than ten. "And these are Thing One, Thing Two, and Thing Three." The kids giggled as she continued, "Otherwise known as Grace, Kelly, and Jimmy."

"There you guys are!" shouted a tall, shaggy-haired guy Liz's age, carrying a bunch of camera gear.

"And that's Big Thing," Liz announced. "Aka Brady. I let him tag along with me sometimes because he's a great action videographer."

"Thanks, sweetie." Brady grinned and kissed her on the cheek. "You really know how to flatter a guy."

"You guys are shooting a ski video at Grand Sky?" I asked.

"Brady's doing the shooting; I'll be giving the kiddos their first ski lessons," she said, resting an arm on Jimmy's shoulder. He and Kelly beamed. Curly-haired Grace looked nearly as terrified as she had when I was about to plow into her.

"That's so cool!" I gushed. "I just hope you don't catch me tumbling down the mountain in the background of any shots."

"Archie Leach saw an article about the documentary we're making on Liz's work with kids in foster care, and he invited us to help break in the slopes. And no one knows how to shred a mountain like Liz," Brady added proudly. "Two-time World Cup gold, *three-time* X Games gold, and she had some of those big-time Team USA girls quaking in their skis before the Olympics a few years ago too."

"Aw, you're gonna make a girl blush," Liz teased, giving him a shove.

"See, that's how you're supposed to flatter a person," Brady asserted.

"It's been a while since I won any medals, though," Liz said, pulling up the leg of her pants to show her scar. "I was on an extreme backcountry ski expedition in the Alps when our chopper crashed. I didn't know if I'd be able to walk at first, let alone ski. Kinda cut my professional career short."

"So she started another one!" Brady said.

"I dreamed about skiing when I was a little kid, but I grew up in the foster-care system in the city, where the only hills we had were covered in concrete," Liz shared. "I'd never even really seen nature before besides a few trees when the family that adopted me moved to the mountains. I got to learn how to ski, and it totally changed my life. So when I wasn't able to ski competitively anymore, I started a nonprofit foundation to give other city kids like me growing up in the foster-care system the same chance I had."

"Yeah, I'm going to win a gold medal at the X Games one day too," Kelly declared.

"Me too!" shouted Jimmy.

"I believe it!" I exclaimed. "That's really amazing, Liz. If there's anything I can do to help, just say the word."

"And she can still ski circles around some of those pros, too!" Brady insisted.

Liz gave him a playful shove toward the door. "Yeah, yeah, stop dawdling, everybody, and let's go find that van. We've got skiing to do!"

I spotted Carol and waved her over, introducing her to Liz's crew as we walked outside.

It wasn't hard to tell which vehicle was there to pick us up. Everyone who passed was taking note of the brand-new hybrid passenger van with the giant Grand Sky Lodge logo waiting by the curb.

"Ahoy, skiers!" a chipper voice shouted as the middle-aged woman driving hopped out and walked around to greet us, jingling oddly as she went.

Or I should say limped around to greet us. She was wearing one of those walking boots they give you when you break a foot or ankle, and she was using a cane. Dangling from the boot was a cute little strand of mini sleigh bells. Big pouffy red earmuffs framed her short hair, and a gaudy Christmas sweater decorated in woven skiers and snowflakes completed her seasonal ensemble.

"Welcome to Montana!" she said cheerily, swinging open the van's back doors. "Toss your gear back here and hop on in. Since your flight was late, we're gonna have to rush to make it back in time."

"Thank—" I barely had the word started before she resumed talking at an impossibly perky, rapid-fire pace.

"I'm Jacqueline, by the way," she declared enthusiastically as she opened the van's passenger doors next. "But everyone calls me Jackie. Or Jackie-of-All-Trades, if you prefer. I'm the lodge's guest services liaison, which is a fancy way of saying I do a little bit of everything. And my job right now is to get you folks to the lodge in time for the big grand opening ceremony at noon!"

"Thanks, Jackie—" I tried to say again, but she bowled right ahead before I could blurt the words out.

"Head count!" she announced, pointing to each of us as she counted aloud. "One, two, three, four, five, six, seven. Perfect! All aboard!"

"Nice to meet you, Jackie!" I chirped (finally able to complete my sentence!) as I climbed in. Jackie was so intensely cheerful, it was hard not to be cheery in response.

"You too, Miss Drew!" She smiled into the rearview mirror. "Mr. A's told us all about how your detecting skills saved the day on that big business case of his. You're practically a celebrity at the lodge!"

I blushed as Liz, Brady, and the kids gave me curious looks.

"Detecting?" Brady inquired.

"Do tell," Liz prodded.

"I have a reputation for solving mysteries back in River Heights, my hometown," I explained. "My dad's a lawyer. I don't usually help him with cases, but this one just sort of fell into my lap. Anyway, Dad represented Archie's firm on a routine real estate case, and I found out the other side wasn't acting fairly, and we were able to get the case settled pretty quickly."

"Don't be modest. Mr. A says your sleuthing personally saved him a fortune. He can't wait to see you again. And he's excited to meet Miss Fremont and Miss Garcia, too," Jackie added, looking at Carol and Liz in her rearview as she drove. "Our grand reopening! This is so exciting!"

"So you worked at the lodge before the big renovation?" Carol asked, notebook open, reporter mode on.

"You betcha! Been working there practically my whole life, and done just about every job there is, from housekeeping to restaurant hostess to ski patrol to concierge."

"That's great they kept you on," Liz said. "A lot of times, old lodges will get gobbled up by a handful of big ski conglomerates, who end up canning all the locals to bring in their own people."

"Leach and Alexander are actually a pretty small development firm," I said. "This is the first ski resort they've owned."

"And kooky old Mrs. Bosley didn't give them a choice," Jackie informed us. "She made sure to put it right there in the contract when they sold the lodge: anyone who wants to stay, can. And just about everyone did. Well, most of us, anyway. Not everyone was happy about the change. The Bosleys' son, Dino, used to be the GM, but he hasn't set foot in the place since Mr. and Mrs. Bos signed the paperwork. Guess he always figured he'd be the one calling the shots one day and didn't like taking orders from someone who wasn't his ma or pa. Not that he liked taking orders from them either. Oops . . ."

Jackie eyed Carol in the rearview. "Probably shouldn't be telling you folks all this. Some people say I'm a gossip, but I say I'm just a people person who likes to talk about the people I know. And I know everybody! Well, everybody in Prospect, at least."

"The Bosleys are the old owners?" I asked.

"Yup. Mrs. Bosley's family owned it for generations going all the way back to Prospect's gold rush days, before tourists ever took to skiing up here. Miners, fur trappers, hunters, lots of trades lodged here before the ski resort became the big thing."

"Doesn't sound like it's been much of a big thing lately," Carol said pointedly. "I heard the Grand Sky hasn't been all that grand for a while."

Jackie nodded sadly. "Hard times. Mr. and Mrs. Bos just didn't have the cash to keep up with the other resorts around here. Like Miss Garcia said, conglomerates have been buying up all the little guys and turning them into big guys, and that makes it hard for the leftover little guys to get by. But we're all sure hoping Mr. A and Mr. G can change that! The Grand Sky was *the* place to be when I was a kid, and I'm just tickled pink to think it can be again."

The van zipped by the vast snow-covered mountain landscape as Jackie talked.

"Did you break your foot skiing?" Grace asked timidly. They were the first words I'd heard her speak.

Jackie guffawed like it was the funniest thing she'd ever heard. "It would be a lot more glamorous if I did! I'd lie and say I broke it on one of the diamonds, but I'm a terrible liar. Truth is I dropped a log on my foot chopping wood for the big opening-night bonfire. It's pretty much the least glam ski lodge accident ever! Luckily, our doctor on the hill, Doc Sherman, was there when it happened and was able to patch me up lickety-split."

"Doctor on the hill?" I asked.

"Resorts usually have a doctor on-site," Liz answered. "They keep a radio on them when they ski so they can triage accidents as soon as a skier goes down."

"Used to be, Doc Sherman would have to transport

you all the way to the local hospital to do any real doctoring, but our new owners put in a state-of-the-art on-site clinic where he can handle just about any routine ski accident right there at the lodge."

The landscape suddenly changed from a narrow, twisty mountain road to a wide-open valley as the van reached the top of a steep hill and headed down the other side toward just about the cutest little ski town you've ever seen.

"Welcome to Prospect, Montana!" Jackie announced.

Looking at it from above as the van rolled down into the valley, you'd think you were staring at a picture-perfect Christmas card. A frontier-style main street with holiday decorations strung between the buildings over the road led straight through the center of town. The flat facades rising over the awnings of the quaint two- and three-story buildings were mostly all joined together like the Old West towns in movies and photographs. If it weren't for the cars and a few traffic lights, you'd almost think you'd traveled back in time to a real prospecting town. Or a snow globe.

With sun shining off the snow-covered rooftops and awnings, the town seemed to sparkle. Shining brightest in the distance a couple of miles beyond the end of Main Street was the Grand Sky Lodge's mountaintop perch. The lodge itself looked tiny from so far away, but there was no way to miss the gleaming white slopes crisscrossing their way down the steep mountain above it.

"Yes!" Brady said.

"Come to mama!" Liz exclaimed, giving him a high five.

"Whoo-hoo!" Kelly and Jimmy yelled, joining in the high-five fest as Grace shrank down in her seat.

"Are they all that tall?" she asked meekly.

"They better not be," I said. "I'm going to be right beside you on the bunny slopes for the first day or two until I get the hang of things."

At the base of the mountain, not far from the lodge, was a small frozen lake. Steam rose into the sky from one end, which was where I guessed the hot springs advertised in the Grand Sky's brochure must be.

"I can see the *Travel Bug* cover now," Carol said, practically drooling.

"I'll tell ya, I'm not as crazy about these cold winters as I used to be when I was y'all's age, but this view never gets old," Jackie shared as the van descended into the valley. "Your friend Jackie's got her eye on trading in snow for sand and retiring to the Caribbean like the Bosleys did, but I sure will miss seeing this when I go."

"It could use a paint job," Carol muttered a few minutes later as the van hit Main Street.

The town was still supercute up close, but you could tell from the chipped paint and a couple of boarded-up storefronts that some of the buildings had seen better days.

"Mr. A has big plans to help renovate the town, too, once the new lodge takes off," Jackie said. "He says having a topflight green ski resort is going to make us an ecotourism hot spot and turn Prospect back into a winter sports paradise."

"What's going on there?" Liz pointed to a large

crowd of angry-looking people holding signs gathered at the end of the street, spilling into the road and blocking traffic. "Some kind of holiday parade?"

"Um, not exactly," Jackie said, her voice a little less cheery than usual.

"It looks like some kind of protest," Brady commented as we got close enough to read some of the signs being waved by the protesters.

SAVE OUR MOUNTAIN . . .

PEOPLE OVER PROFITS . . .

THERE IS NO PLANET B . . .

STOP THE PIPELINE . . .

OIL SPILLS KILL . . . This last one had drawings of dead fish with *X*s for eyes and a kitchen sink with a poison symbol dripping out of it.

Traffic had come to a halt and people were honking. Some of them gave thumbs-up to show their support for the protesters. Others screamed out their windows for the people to get out of the way.

Protesters weren't the only people gathering along Main Street, though. A row of police officers in full riot gear were lined up on the other side of the street, guarding the Prospect town hall. More officers were escorting a group of men and women in a mixture of business attire and ski wear out of the building and shielding them from jeering protesters.

At least one of the men didn't look like he needed the extra protection, though. He had on a perfectly tailored pin-striped designer overcoat that was a lot more Wall Street than Main Street. The expensive coat was accessorized by a silk scarf—and two hulking bodyguards of his own.

Most of the others exiting the building looked less conspicuous, including one man I recognized from his picture as Montana state representative Grant Alexander, aka Archie's real estate partner and co-owner of the Big Sky Lodge.

Carol had her phone out and was eagerly snapping pictures through the window, a sly smile on her face. "Looks like trouble in paradise to me."

CHAPTER TWO

~

A Real Winter Wonderland

SOME OF THE CHEER DRAINED OUT OF Jackie as she drove past the protest.

"All the land for miles surrounding the mountain that wasn't owned by the lodge or town folks used to be a protected wilderness preserve. Some of the most beautiful country you've ever seen, and the state had promised to keep it that way forever. . . ." Jackie frowned. "Until last year, when the government opened it up to oil and gas exploration. Next thing you knew, we had all these Big Oil vultures circling so they could build a new pipeline to move their crude oil right through our valley on its way south from Canada."

Jackie shook her head in dismay at the town hall. But somehow even sad Jackie still managed to sound chipper.

Liz didn't, though. "There's not that much pristine nature left. Why are people determined to destroy it? How many oil spills do there have to be before we stop letting them do this?"

Oil pipelines and the controversies they caused had been big news recently. There were already thousands and thousands of miles of pipes transporting oil and natural gas all over the country, and constructing new ones caused all kinds of environmental risks, especially if anything ever went wrong. And not just to plants and animals, either, which was bad enough, but also to the people who depended on water and soil that could become polluted if there were ever a leak.

"Can't the town stop it?" I asked.

"The town wants it!" Jackie said. "Or at least enough people do that the town council voted to approve it.

That's some of them leaving the hall now, along with the oil fat cats and poor Mr. G."

"Grant Alexander is supporting the pipeline?" I asked incredulously. The co-owner of an eco-resort supporting an oil pipeline would be like . . . like . . . well, something really bad that I couldn't even think of because it made me so mad!

"Mr. G is just caught in the middle. Literally!" Jackie exclaimed. "A sliver of the land the pipeline needs cuts right across the edge of Grand Sky's property. Construction would have started already if Mr. A and Mr. L hadn't refused to lease it to them. A ski lodge with a big ugly ol' oil pipeline running through it wouldn't be much of an eco-resort, would it?" Jackie's grin was back. "I happen to agree with them, but not all the town folks feel the same. The lodge isn't just standing in the way of the pipeline. The pipeline company is promising a lot of folks good money, and truth is, a lot of them could use it. There's supposed to be all kinds of construction jobs, and some of our neighbors could lose a pretty penny on land leases if the pipeline has to go somewhere else, Dino Bosley and our esteemed sheriff included."

Jackie nodded out the window at the police in riot gear as the van passed.

"That must be a tough position for Mr. Alexander to be in as both a state representative and a business owner," I observed.

"It'll lose him some votes and win him others, but I don't envy him. He's got a lot of grumpier-than-usual constituents who want this deal done, both in Prospect and across the district." She lowered her voice confidentially. "Now I'm not one to spread rumors, but I heard they've both received death threats!"

The words gave me shivers, and from the gasps in the row behind me, everyone else had them too. I had the impression that Carol's were more excited than shocked, though. I saw her eagerly take notes in the seat beside me. I wasn't sure this was the type of publicity Archie was hoping for when he invited a writer from *Travel Bug*.

I turned to watch the protest grow smaller behind

us as we left town and headed uphill toward the lodge. Detecting teaches you to be objective and not jump to conclusions until you have all the facts, but it was hard not to root for the Prospect pipeline protesters. There was even a small group of what looked like high school students right at the front, taking a stand for something they believed in. Two guys held up a peculiar banner that read GECCOS AGAINST GLOBAL WARMING. I had no idea what "Geccos" were, except maybe a misspelled type of lizard. One of the guys had brown hair and the other blond, and they looked oddly familiar, although I couldn't quite place them.

Jackie's perky voice drew my attention back to the view in front of us.

"We're almost there!" she said.

The Grand Sky grew larger ahead of us. It had the feel of a quintessential Western log hunting lodge. Except way bigger. The main lodge itself was two stories tall, with towering glass windows in front. Breezeways connected it to smaller lodges on either side in a horseshoe shape, and there were a bunch of log buildings of different sizes laid out on the hill below it like a little log cabin village. You could tell the main lodge in the center was the oldest, but it had been beautifully restored, and all the other structures were built in the same Old West log cabin style.

Steam rose from the hot springs near the lake off to the side, and a wall of evergreen hedges strung with Christmas decorations framed either side of the lodge's arched gates. As we drove through, you could see the tiny-looking skiers congregating at the base of the slopes just above the lodge and riding the ski lifts up to the top.

"The conditions look perfect, and no one's even laid down any tracks yet!" Liz proclaimed.

"Nope!" replied Jackie. "Mr. A wanted to make sure you guys were some of the first! Speaking of which . . ." She glanced at the dashboard clock. "The opening ceremony starts in less than an hour!"

Jackie slammed on the accelerator, rocketing the van up the hill to the front of the lodge. Well, at least as fast as a hybrid van could rocket, and without endangering anyone, anyway!

"Now, normally I'd give you folks a whole spiel on the lodge's history and where everything is, but I have strict orders to make sure Liz is suited up in time for the ceremonial first run." Jackie climbed out of the van and limped over to the cargo doors, jingling and talking nonstop as she went. "We're going to send a skier or a snowboarder down every single slope at the same time while a drone films it all! And Miss Garcia gets to go down our steepest double black diamond! It's not every day we get a multiple gold medalist staying with us!"

"Yes!" Liz pumped her fist.

"Can I send my drone up to film it too?" asked Brady.

Jackie winked. "It's your drone Mr. A planned to use to shoot everything. He wanted to surprise you guys with the news himself, but your plane's late arrival has had to rush the plan along."

"No problem! This is going to be awesome," Brady replied.

"Grab your gear and follow me to the locker rooms," Jackie said, then turned to me and Carol. "Mr. A wasn't sure if you guys would have your own gear, so he's got the rental shop on call with our best kits waiting. He didn't want to put you on the spot, so you can watch the first run from the top and then pick whichever trail you want when you're ready. Ooh! We're all so excited to have you write about our big reopening, Miss Fremont! Do you think you could interview me?"

Carol chuckled. "I think I just did."

Jackie looked a little confused but beamed nonetheless. "Okay, then! Let's hit the slopes!"

We were in a rush, so I didn't get to linger, but the lodge was just as impressive on the inside. There were tons of exposed logs and stone, big, bright windows, comfy-looking dark leather furniture, and cozy fireplaces. And Christmas trees! There was a tree and a menorah in just about every space we walked through. There was no mistaking what season it was.

The walls were decorated with a mixture of antique

skiing, hunting, fishing, fur-trapping, and mining memorabilia from the lodge's past. A lot of care had obviously been taken to preserve a real sense of local Montana history; it was almost like a frontier museum you could live in. Just a lot more luxurious than the real frontier was, thankfully.

Stepping from the lodge itself into the state-of-the-art Grand Sky Ski Shop & Demo Center behind it was like stepping from the early 1900s back into the twenty-first century. The center was as modern as the rest of the lodge's decor was historical. The amount of equipment was overwhelming. I never would have known where to even begin picking out the right gear on my own.

Luckily, I didn't have to. The manager had a full package already selected for me and ready to go, just like Jackie promised. Skis, poles, boots, a helmet, goggles, gloves, and a super-warm-looking ski pants/jacket combo stitched with the Grand Sky logo. They even had sunscreen for the little bit of skin I still had exposed once I was suited up. It might seem weird to worry about getting sunburn in the snow, but when the sun's out, all that snow acts like a giant reflector. Without the goggles' reflective lenses and the sunscreen, I might go snow-blind *and* turn red as a lobster!

Liz had already headed for the slopes by the time Carol and I were suited up. Jackie saw us off at the door.

"Sorry I won't be joining you," she said, jingling the little bells on her walking boot as explanation. "Have fun! I'll see you in the ski lounge for hot chocolate when you're done!"

The view from the ski lift was breathtaking. The mountain rose above me, and looking behind us, you could see the whole lodge and clear across the entire valley and the town of Prospect a few miles below. I remembered I wasn't just looking at Montana—I could see into Wyoming, too. According to the brochure, the lodge was perfectly perched so you could actually ski from one state into the other if you wanted.

The mountain itself was covered with snow-dusted

pine trees anywhere there wasn't a ski slope. I could even see Brady's drone zipping by overhead. I gave a big grin and waved, wondering whether the camera could see me.

From way up here, I could tell that the wall of evergreen hedges framing the lodge's entry gates was actually the edge of a huge, intricate maze made out of trimmed hedges. I'd seen one that looked a lot like it at a mountain resort in *The Shining*, one of George's favorite movies. Watching that had been a huge mistake. Give me a real-life bad guy over a scary horror-movie bad guy any day! Anyway, what I learned from *The Shining* is basically, never go into a maze of hedges unless you want to get lost and possibly chopped up by an ax murderer. So, yeah, I probably wouldn't be going in there during my stay at the Grand Sky Lodge.

A crowd of people was gathered when I reached the top of the ski lift. This one ended midway up the mountain on a relatively flat area, where a few of the trails intersected and continued down the mountain. Other lifts brought you higher up to the more advanced slopes.

I looked around at the dramatic landscape, relieved that I wasn't part of the inaugural first run. I hadn't been on a pair of skis for a while and figured it would be good just to watch for a bit to refresh my memory before slowly making my way down one of these easier trails.

"There she is!" a familiar voice called.

I turned around to see a middle-aged man with a handsome, boyish face and a slightly goofy grin waving me over to a spot in the center where a large group of skiers had gathered.

"Hi, Archie!" I called, scooting myself over to him with my ski poles. "Thanks so much for inviting us. This place is fantastic!"

"It's my pleasure, Nancy! I really can't thank you or your dad enough. If it hadn't been for your detective work and your dad's legal skills, we might have been trapped in that contract. And then who knows where we'd be? Hey, where is Carson?" he asked, looking around for my dad. "I have some exciting conservation plans for the lodge I'd like to get his legal advice on while he's here."

"He had an important last-minute deposition back in River Heights and had to change his flight, but he should be here tomorrow," I filled him in as Carol slid up next to me. "But I did get to sit next to another one of your guests on the plane instead. This is Carol Fremont from *Travel Bug*."

"Impressive place, Mr. Leach," Carol said.

"Just Archie, please!" he insisted. "I am so glad you could make it! We're thrilled that *Travel Bug* wants to do a feature on us. I think we're on the cutting edge of a movement that could change how people think about responsible tourism as a way to make a lasting impact on the planet and have fun at the same time. I was just about to kick off the festivities with a few words about our mission, but before I do, I have another little mystery I was hoping Nancy might be able to help me resolve."

My ears perked right up at that. "I'll do anything I can to help. I'm always down to solve a mystery."

"You heard about our plan to send a skier down every slope all at once for the inaugural first run, right?" he asked, and I nodded. "Well, our wonderful new chef was supposed to be one of the honorary first skiers, but she's refused to leave her kitchen until all the prep for our big opening-night banquet is done. Which means we're missing a skier. And I'd hoped my favorite young detective might do the lodge the honor of taking her place."

So much for my plan to wait and watch before taking my first plunge.

"Um, this case might be harder than it sounds," I said. "I'm a lot more confident in my detecting abilities than my skiing. It's been a while since I've put on a pair of skis, and I'm feeling a little rusty. I don't want to ruin your video by rolling all the way down the hill!"

Archie laughed. "Then it's a good thing it's one of our easiest trails you'll be skiing. A smooth grade all the way down with no big turns, hazards, or moguls. Our grooming crew was out early this morning marking icy patches to make sure all our bunny slopes are safe for beginners. It'll be the perfect run to warm you up for a week of great skiing."

I was still a little nervous, but I wasn't about to turn down a challenge. Or let Archie down, for that matter. Besides, it was just a bunny hill. What could go wrong?

I smiled. How could I say no? "Count me in."

"Wonderful! Now if you ladies will excuse me for a minute." Archie took a wireless microphone from one of the people he'd been talking to just as Grant Alexander skied up alongside him.

"Ah, just in time, Grant," Archie said, clicking on the mic and turning to the crowd. "Ladies and gentlemen, welcome to the grand reopening of the Grand Sky Lodge, one of Montana's oldest ski lodges, and now its greenest as well!"

A round of applause went up from the crowd.

"By using renewable energy sources that reduce our dependence on fossil fuels, locally sourced goods that require less fuel to transport *and* support neighboring businesses, and sustainable products that produce less waste, Grand Sky will have a carbon footprint smaller than a resort half our size!" Archie continued. "And unlike most tourism businesses, we don't just use resources, we create them—from the solar energy we generate to light our lodge to the thousands of pounds of composted food waste that we transform into the soil our world-famous chef Kim Crockett uses to grow the vegetables served in our exquisite new fine dining destination, Mountain to Table. I hope to see many of you tonight at our opening-night banquet, where you'll get to sample some of her magnificent culinary creations."

"Whoo-hoo!" I shouted, cheering along with everyone else.

"Transforming the Grand Sky into a truly environmentally friendly resort didn't come cheap," Archie informed the crowd. "As our investors keep reminding us, it would have been a lot less expensive just to do things the old-fashioned wasteful way, but I've always believed in putting my money where my mouth is."

Grant leaned over to speak into the mic. "He put my money where his mouth is too!"

The joke got a big laugh from the crowd, Archie included.

"It's true. My longtime friend and business partner, Representative Alexander, is living proof that not all politicians are greedy," Archie said, earning another laugh. "We both have a lot riding on this vision, but I believe it will pay off for *all* of us in the future. Not just in the money it will save the lodge in operating costs, but in how it can help save the planet. We set out to give people a place where they can have fun in the snow and protect the natural beauty surrounding us at the same time."

There were more cheers as Archie continued.

"But we're not just putting our money where our mouths are, we're putting our land there too. As some of you know, the lodge owns hundreds of acres of pristine, undeveloped backcountry surrounding our ski slopes. To help achieve our goal, I intend to create a forever wild conservancy to protect that land and ensure that it can never be developed or exploited by anyone, not even by us. Our guests will be able to ski, hike, and enjoy every inch of the preserve's beauty, but nothing bigger than a campfire will ever be built on it."

Everyone clapped, but the biggest cheer went up from the back of the crowd. I turned around to see a few more familiar faces. They'd ditched the signs, but a number of the protesters must have rushed over from the town hall, including the two high school kids I'd seen with the GECCOS sign.

"Does that include the land the pipeline wants to build on?" Carol asked from the front, back in full-on reporter mode. It was the same question my detective brain would have asked if there'd been a mystery to investigate.

Archie smiled, but Grant reached in and grabbed the mic before he had a chance to reply.

"Wow, Arch, I think you surprised all of us with that one," he said.

His tone was joking, but he looked like he'd suddenly gone a shade paler. Considering that Grant was a politician, I didn't blame him. Archie's land conservancy idea could shut down the pipeline for good, and if Grant really hadn't known about it, Archie had just dropped a huge political hot potato in his lap. It probably wasn't going to make whoever was sending those death threats very happy either.

"I think one thing my partner forgot to mention with all the talk of food waste and compost is the world-class skiing!" Grant continued, quickly changing the topic. "I've built my career as a politician on bringing prosperity back to great towns like Prospect and to all the good, hardworking folks in my district. Turning Grand Sky Lodge back into one of the premiere ski destinations in Montana is going to be a huge boost to the local economy and a grand achievement everyone in Prospect can be proud of."

Grant paused while the audience cheered.

He went on, "And don't forget to try the restaurants, shops, spa, and all the other great outdoor activities we offer while you're here. Every dollar you spend at the Grand Sky Lodge helps turn Prospect back into the thriving outdoor sports tourism destination it was before and will soon be again. Now let's hit the slopes!"

Grant handed off the microphone to someone as the crowd clapped, and he was quickly surrounded by guests wanting to talk to him. I could see Archie not far off, already schmoozing with skiers as well.

"This story keeps getting better. Nothing like a hot controversy to grab eyeballs," Carol said as she skied off in the other direction.

"Hi, Nancy?" a friendly voice said behind me before I could process what it all might mean for Archie and the lodge. I turned to see a woman in her twenties. She had the same effortless girl-next-door beauty as my friend Bess, only instead of a perfectly put-together outfit, she was wearing a red ski jacket with a wireless radio receiver strapped to one of the chest pockets and a large white cross with the words SKI PATROL on the other. Her dark hair was twisted into a long, thick braid that hung down her back from the base of her helmet.

"I'm Marni," she said. "I'm with the ski patrol. Archie asked me to show you to your slope for the opening run. Once everybody's lined up, they're going to send up a flare so all the skiers can head down at the same time."

"I just hope I don't ruin the shot," I half joked.

"Don't even worry—the hill you're going down is a breeze," Marni assured me. "Besides, I can tell from the way you balance on your skis, you're already ready for a more advanced run than this one. You're going to kill it."

"Thanks, Marni!" I was feeling a lot better about everything; her confidence was just what I needed.

Everybody knew ski patrollers were basically the rock stars of the slopes, with the most glamorous—and dangerous—job on the mountain. They were the fearless heroes who swooped in to rescue people when they skied off a cliff or got trapped in an avalanche—not that I was going to get caught in an avalanche on a bunny slope. But Marni had the same professional self-assurance I'd noticed in Liz, and her encouragement had me feeling more confident too.

A few minutes later I was lined up, staring down my first run of the day. I was feeling steadier on my skis already. And the trail looked just like Archie had said, a smooth run to the bottom without any big twists or obstacles. My dreams of conquering double black diamonds were returning. I was ready to coast through run number one and move on to something more challenging!

"This slope has some pretty deep drifts off to the side, so it's rated a little higher than most of our beginner trails, but really just as a safety precaution," Marni said, pointing to a tall snowbank a few yards past a large orange sign that read SKI BOUNDARY AREA—NO SKIING BEYOND THIS POINT. "But the borders are clearly marked and the run is a breeze. There's only one small curve halfway down, and it's wide enough you barely have to turn. Just stay away from the red flags, where it can get icy, and you'll be fine."

"Thanks, Marni," I said. "I feel like I have my own private ski coach."

Marni smiled. "We're going to have you skiing like you were doing it your whole life before you leave here. . . . There it is!"

She pointed at the bright red flare rising over the mountain.

"Let's do this!" I shouted, pushing myself off with my poles and shooting down the hill.

Okay, maybe "shooting" was an overstatement. I was coasting at a leisurely pace, but I felt great! The snow was perfectly powdery, I had my weight balanced forward over my skis just like you're supposed to, and the view down the mountain was glorious. Archie and Marni were right—the slope was a breeze, and I found myself wishing I could go even faster and really feel the wind whipping against my face. Maybe I really would be carving up diamonds and making jumps before the week was out!

I was gliding toward the bend when I saw a couple of the red ice markers Marni had mentioned planted in the snow in the middle of the slope to warn me away from the left side. It made the trail a lot narrower than I expected heading into the bend and forced me closer to the boundary signs to my right, but it really wasn't much of a turn and I still had plenty of room. I leaned gently into the curve, shifting my weight to steer myself left.

That's when I felt the soft powder under my skis turn to solid ice. My speed doubled in an instant and my center of gravity was totally thrown off. I tried to catch my balance, but I was no match for the speed, and my skis shot out from under my feet, sending me flying out of control straight toward the ski boundary warning sign!

CHAPTER THREE

~

On Thin
Ice

I WATCHED THE WORDS SKI BOUNDARY AREA—NO
SKIING BEYOND THIS POINT flash by in a blur as I careened
off the trail toward a ten-foot-tall wall of drifted snow.
I braced myself for the impact, but the snow wall caved
under my weight, swallowing me up whole like it was
made of quicksand as I tumbled end over end into a
cold, dark sea of snow.

I came to a painful stop a few seconds later. I wasn't
sure how deep into the drift I'd fallen, but it couldn't
have been more than a few yards. That's what I hoped,
at least. It had been bright and sunny a moment earlier,

but it was so dark inside the snowbank, I could hardly tell if my eyes were open or closed, let alone where I was! I was going to have to feel my way out.

I opened my mouth to take a deep breath and collect myself, only to suck in a mouthful of snow. And that's when I began to get nervous. So I started to dig. It only took me a few feet to realize I had no idea which way I was digging! I wanted to dig my way out, but for all I knew I was just digging myself deeper in . . . or farther down . . . or sideways, for that matter. I'd spun around so many times that I was totally disoriented! And buried! It was like that awful feeling when you get wiped out by a wave at the beach and you can't tell which way is up. I might not be able to drown like I could in the ocean, but I could suffocate. Every time I took a breath, I sucked in more snow.

Calm down, Nancy, you've faced scarier situations than this, I told myself. I'd been in enough close calls to know that just about the worst thing you can do in a crisis is panic. *Stay calm, try to get your bearings, and then you can figure out what to do next.*

I did my best to slow my breathing, inhaling carefully so I didn't choke on the snow while I cleared an air pocket around my face big enough to breathe freely without feeling like I was kissing a snow cone.

That's when I noticed the snow starting to melt from my breath and drip down my chin. Which meant I knew which way was up! Thanks to gravity, you can be pretty sure water isn't going to drip up. I still might not know which way was forward, but if I could crawl up, I'd eventually reach the surface. And freedom.

I had just begun to calmly dig toward the surface when I heard a faint voice. I strained to listen as it got louder. It was calling my name!

It seemed to be coming from in front of me, so I started digging forward. A minute later a hand gripped my wrist and pulled me to the surface.

Sunlight streamed into my face, temporarily blinding me. I'd never been happier to see spots!

"Are you okay, Nancy?" a blurry figure with Marni's voice asked as I blinked the floating spots away.

"I am now . . . ," I started to say, but that was when the adrenaline wore off and the pain kicked in.

"Or maybe not," I squeaked as a white-hot jolt shot through my lower left leg. "I think I might have hurt my ankle."

"Just stay still and let us take care of you," Marni reassured me. "We'll have you back at the lodge in no time. My partner, Berkley, is on the way with the rescue sled. We're gonna give you a chauffeured ride back."

"The sled ride of shame," I groaned. "On my first day, too, *and* on the easy slope. I guess my dreams of Olympic gold will have to wait."

"I'm so sorry, Nancy. I don't know what happened. I've been patrolling these slopes for years, and I've never seen a solid patch of ice like that spread across one of our beginner trails before," Marni said, scrunching her brow. "I don't know why the ice markers are in the middle of the trail instead of there, but with them cutting off the slope, there was no way for you to miss it. If it makes you feel any better, I nearly wiped out coming down after you."

"It kind of does a little, actually." I tried to laugh, but it came out as more of a moan.

Marni smiled as her radio beeped.

"How's she doing, Marni?" a staticky voice buzzed.

"Might be a broken ankle, but she's a trouper," Marni said into her radio, giving me a warm smile. "Let's get the grooming staff down here ASAP. I don't know who put the markers down or how they could've missed a solid sheet of ice right in the middle of the run, but we need to get this trail closed until it's safe."

"Copy that," the voice said, and buzzed off.

"At least I was the one who found the ice and not a little kid," I said, reminding myself that even bad luck can have a silver lining. The accident could have been a whole lot worse if someone like little Grace had wiped out instead of me.

"With that attitude, we're going to have to make you an honorary ski patroller," Marni said, tossing her long braid back over her shoulder.

A few minutes later Marni and her partner, Berkley, had me strapped into a bright orange rescue toboggan, with a wooden splint bracing my left leg and a warm blanket wrapped around me. I saw Brady's drone flying overhead and wondered if he was recording my embarrassing ride down the mountain so the whole world could watch the amateur who busted her leg on her first run on the easy slope. I was pretty sure this wasn't how Archie had hoped the video of his ceremonial first run would end.

Berkley hit the button on his radio. "Berkley here. Let Doc and the clinic know we're on our way in with their first patient."

"Copy that, Berk. Out," a voice buzzed back.

There was a burst of static, and then another, fuzzier voice came on midsentence. And this one was mad. *Screaming* mad. "*. . . still make it work for us, so figure something out fast! Or do I have to tell you how to do everything? I don't want to see them anywhere near . . .*"

"Sorry about that," Berkley said, switching off the radio. "We've got a new radio system, and there are still some kinks with private channels getting crossed."

I had no idea what the person on the radio had

been talking about. The voice sounded vaguely familiar, but I couldn't quite place it.

That wasn't the only yelling we heard on the way down to the clinic.

"Oh, man, I hope Todd doesn't lose his job over this," Berkley said as he and Marni skied my sad little orange rescue toboggan off the slopes past the clubhouse, where a big guy with a beard was yelling at a short guy with a baby face.

"First you slack off, then you have the nerve to lie to me about it?!" the big guy shouted down at the short one.

"I swear, Steve, it's not my fault!" the short one pleaded, hands pressed to his chest like he was praying. "I skied it myself before we did the final pass, and it was perfect. You know I never—"

"All I know is that you had orders you didn't follow, and this is the last time . . ." The big guy's voice faded behind us as we moved farther away.

"I take it Todd is the groomer," I said to my ski patrol chauffeurs, glad to have a tiny mystery to take my mind off my throbbing leg.

"One of them," Berkley answered. "He's in charge of the beginner and intermediate runs on the lower part of the mountain. Big Steve's the head groomer, and he has a temper even when things go right."

"I'd feel terrible if someone got fired because I wiped out," I said, feeling a sting of guilt along with the pain in my leg.

"It's not your fault, Nancy," Marni assured me. "Todd's a good guy, but he really should have flagged that ice. Even the best grooming crew in the world can't catch it all, but there was a solid sheet under the powder covering that whole side of the run by the turn, and the markers they did put down steered you right toward it. It was an accident waiting to happen."

Berkley nodded. "If they'd done a test run like they were supposed to before the opening ceremony, they probably would have caught it."

At the clinic, Berkley and Marni carefully transferred me onto a gurney and wheeled me into an examination room. The clinic was like part emergency room and part high-end spa. The Grand Sky Lodge did hospitality right. The staff was every bit as nice as Marni, Berkley, and Jackie had been. Well, maybe not all the staff.

Doc Sherman was a jumpy middle-aged man with sandy brown hair that was starting to gray, wire-rim glasses, and just about the least confidence-inspiring bedside manner I'd ever seen from a doctor. It's not that he said anything mean—he didn't say much at all, really—he was just a lot more fidgety and grouchy-looking than you hope to see from a guy who sometimes operates on people.

"Hmm," "Mm-hmm," and "Huh" seemed to make up most of his vocabulary as he examined me. His other favorite words were, "Does this hurt?"

"Ouch!" I said as he poked the fresh bruise below my hip a bit too hard. "It's a little sore, I guess, but I didn't really notice so much until you poked it."

"Hmm," he replied, and got up and left the room, sending an older nurse named Mariana in after him to take me down the hall for X-rays.

"I'm sorry, dear. Doc Sherman isn't usually this grumpy," Mariana said, leaning in and lowering her voice to a whisper as she pushed me back to the exam room in a wheelchair. "He's got a boil on his rear end that's been giving him fits. Don't tell anyone."

I laughed. Doc Sourpuss with a boil on his butt did make me feel a little better. It didn't last long, though.

Doc Sourpuss walked in with two X-rays in his hand. He put the first one up on the light box. There were my lower left leg and foot bones in all their black-and-white film-negative glory.

"That's your tibia," he said, pointing to the bone just above where my ski boot had been. "And that"—he indicated a little squiggly-looking spot on the bone—"is a small hairline fracture."

"Ugh," I groaned, seeing my would-be glorious week of skiing flash before my eyes. *At least it's only a small fracture,* I thought, reassuring myself.

"That's the good news," he said.

My mouth dropped open. "Huh?"

He slapped the second X-ray onto the light box.

This one showed the long bone connecting my hip and my knee, and the thing he was pointing to below my hip wasn't a faint squiggly line. It looked like someone had snipped the bone cleanly in two with scissors!

"You have a femoral fracture," he declared.

"But—but—" I stammered. "It was just a little bruise."

"Appearances can be misleading," he said. It would have been good detecting advice, but I didn't much appreciate it as a medical patient.

"You're lucky it doesn't require surgery," he continued. "But we are going to have to immobilize it immediately."

I quickly learned that by "immobilize," he meant a cast—and not just one of those walking boots like jingly Jackie had that lets you still move around everywhere, but a huge foot-to-thigh behemoth cast that made me look like a mummy someone had forgotten to finish wrapping!

As if that wasn't bad enough . . .

"You need to stay off it entirely for the next week,"

he declared like a judge reading a prison sentence to a convict.

"But—but—" I stammered again.

"You can have a wheelchair in case you need to go anywhere, although I don't recommend it," he warned. "In fact, I recommend total bed rest."

"B-but—" I stammered some more.

"Don't even consider trying to put weight on it," he said, ignoring my gibbering. "If it heals properly, we can replace the cast with a less cumbersome brace before you leave and send you home on crutches."

"But I just got here!" I finally spit out. "And it barely even hurts!"

"The protruding bone appears to have hit a nerve, causing localized numbing," he explained impatiently. "But if you don't keep it entirely immobile during the first seven days of the crucial healing stage, then you could leave here with nerve damage and a permanent limp. Stay off it."

Mic drop. Exit stage left. Or at least that's how I envisioned it as Doc Sherman set his clipboard down on the desk and walked out of the room chewing on his lip, leaving me to contemplate the reality of his verdict.

The dream ski vacation I'd been so excited for? I was going to be spending the entire thing watching everyone else have fun skiing while I was stuck indoors in a cast!

CHAPTER FOUR

A Room with a View

I HAD TO ADMIT, THERE WERE WORSE places to be stuck in bed than a corner suite at the Grand Sky Lodge. Archie had booked my dad and me into a beautiful suite with a living room, two bedrooms, three fireplaces, and one fantastic view. Well, actually, *three* fantastic views. Because it was on the corner, each room offered its own breathtaking panorama. I could look out over either the front of the lodge, all the way down to Prospect and the valley below, or up at the ski-slope-covered mountains, depending on where I wheeled myself. Plus, the suite was only two floors up, so I could look down to the courtyard and hedge maze below. I was in perfect people-watching position.

Okay, so I know Dr. Sherman had recommended bed rest, but I told myself it was only a recommendation, after all. I mean, it wasn't like he'd given me an order or anything. My upper leg really didn't hurt much at all; I mostly just felt a throbbing in my lower shin where I'd broken my tibia. If anything, I felt drowsy from the pain medication they'd given me. And with the huge, bulky cast, it was actually less uncomfortable sitting in my wheelchair with my left leg stretched out in front of me than lying in bed anyway. I was sure the doctor would want me to be comfortable—that certainly seemed like an important medical consideration too. And, besides, just thinking about being stuck in bed for a whole week while I was in this amazing place made me stir-crazy! I figured being able to wheel myself around was actually an important mental health consideration. Surely the doctor wouldn't want me going *crazy*, right?! I'd just be super careful not to jostle my cast too much or bang into anything. I was determined not to let a little thing like a badly broken leg ruin my vacation!

Archie had felt so bad about my accident that he made me feel bad for him. I tried to assure him that it really wasn't his fault and just bad luck, but he was convinced I never would have gotten hurt if it hadn't been for him asking me to sub in for the ceremonial first run. He insisted on giving me anything and everything I might need to make myself comfortable, including my own personal walkie-talkie radio to communicate with the staff and a really nice pair of binoculars to watch the action on the slopes. Not that watching everybody else having a blast skiing while I was stuck inside in a cast was my idea of the most fun activity ever, but it sure beat staring at the walls (although the exposed log walls with their rustic built-in breakfast nook and benches were pretty nice!).

Liz had cut her skiing short and rushed up to the suite to see me as soon as she heard what happened from Brady, who really had caught the whole embarrassing mishap on his drone cam. Things One through Three insisted on being the first ones to sign my ginormo cast, and Liz got right down to business teaching me how to maneuver my wheelchair around.

"Believe me, doll, I know," she said, tapping the boot of her scarred leg with authority. "I spent a lot of time in one of those when I was rehabbing after the helicopter crash."

Liz was a great teacher, and I was excited to use my binoculars to watch her giving the kids their ski lessons later. I had to tell Kelly and Jimmy that I wasn't quite ready for wheelies, but we all agreed that Liz should show me tips for what she called "stealth mode" so I wouldn't make a racket everywhere I went.

"You're not going to be able to spy on any perps squeaking everywhere you go and banging into walls," Liz pointed out.

"Now I just need a case to solve!" I said, laughing.

I was actually having fun! Even though I was bummed that my dad wasn't there yet, and I missed George, Bess, and my boyfriend, Ned, I definitely wasn't lonely. Breaking your leg the first day on the slopes still stinks, but it stinks a lot less with friends to cheer you up.

Everyone was supersweet and concerned. Carol took a selfie of us to post on Instagram with the hashtags #traveltips and #hownottostartyourskitrip. Jackie jingled by the suite to fret over me not staying in bed and to bring me a pair of matching mini sleigh bells for my wheelchair so we could be "twinsies," as she put it. I told her I'd hang them from the door of the suite and think of her every time I came and went. I might not be on an active investigation, but you never knew when one might come up. Wheelchair or no, I was still a detective, and snooping gets a lot harder when people can hear you coming from around the corner.

Eventually everyone left to let me rest. But I was still too wired from all the excitement to do any napping, so I picked up my brand-new binoculars to get a better look at the Grand Sky's grounds.

It took me only a second to realize that I didn't just have a great view of the slopes and the valley. I also had a clear view of a lot of the other rooms. The hotel part of the lodge was horseshoe-shaped, and from where we were, I could see all the other rooms on the front side of the lodge, along with some of the private cabins spread out on the hill below.

It was getting late in the day, and I'd meant to watch the last ski runs before the sun set, but the view of the other rooms proved too tempting not to investigate. I couldn't ski or hike or ice-skate on the frozen pond or most of the other winter activities the lodge offered, but you didn't need to be able to walk around to sleuth.

I just had to figure out what I was sleuthing for. The pipeline controversy seemed like a good prospect, but it wasn't like anyone had been kidnapped or anything. Then again, there *were* the death threats against Grant and Leach that Jackie had told us about. Now that was a promising angle.

After all, it doesn't get much more serious than a death threat! One of the people who made the threats could be staying at the lodge. I kind of had an obligation to conduct at least cursory surveillance. That's what I tried to tell myself, at least.

Nope! I scolded myself. *No snooping without probable cause!*

I was lowering my binoculars when I caught sight of two men arguing in one of the second-floor corner suites on the opposite side of the horseshoe. My hands slowed down instinctively as Archie and Grant came into clear focus.

Now *this* was directly relevant to the death-threat case I'd just assigned to myself. If Jackie was right, and someone had been threatening Archie and Grant, a good way to get a bead on suspects or their motives would be to observe their victims. As co-owners of the resort that was standing in the way of the pipeline being built, they were both in the pipeline proponents' crosshairs. Which meant they could both be in danger.

The binoculars were pretty powerful, but I was still too far away to read their lips. It was obvious that they were both pretty worked up, though.

It wasn't shocking that there was tension between Archie and Grant, especially after the surprise Archie had dropped in his opening-ceremony comments about wanting to turn the land around the lodge—including the disputed sliver of land needed by the pipeline—into a permanent nature preserve that would stop the pipeline in its tracks. Grant was in the tricky position of not only opposing the pipeline as an owner of the lodge, but also, as a state politician, not wanting to offend the constituents who supported it—and it looked like Archie had just made that job a lot harder.

It was hard to tell who was angrier at whom, though. Archie was waving his hands and Grant was waving a document. He tried to force it into Archie's hands, but Archie pushed it away and stormed out. I could see Grant throw the papers down and sit in a chair after Archie marched out. It was tempting to try and read into what the argument might be about, but it really could have been about anything. They were business partners on the opening day of their company's biggest—and from the way it sounded at the opening ceremony, riskiest—investment, and they both had a lot riding on its success. No wonder they were tense. The argument could have been over financing or which brand of recycled toilet tissue they were buying, for all I knew.

What I did know was that I was *tired*.

KNOCK. KNOCK.

I woke up to a fist knocking on my suite door a couple of hours later. I must have fallen asleep in the wheelchair.

"The butler did it!" I shouted in confusion from somewhere deep in dreamland. "Um . . ." I cleared my throat. "Who is it?"

"Dinnertime, sleepyhead!" Liz's voice shouted from the other side of the door. "I hear that fancy-pants chef you were talking about has a heck of a feast planned, and I didn't want a little bit of bad luck to stop you from chowing down!"

"Coming!" I shouted back. Doc Sherman may have prescribed rest, but I wasn't about to miss this. I wheeled myself over to the door, narrowly avoiding a collision between my cast and the wall as I swiveled around to try and open it.

"We need to work on your stealth mode moves," Liz said from the other side of the door. "I can hear you from across the suite."

I opened the door for her. "Come on in!" I welcomed her.

She was wearing an awesome black jumpsuit with leopard-print ankle boots. Her hair was pulled back to show off a pair of glittering Christmas tree earrings, complete with tiny golden stars. I looked down at my black leggings and purple fleece with dismay.

"You look great, Liz!" I told her. "I'm a little worried this outfit doesn't say 'grand opening,' though. . . ."

"That's why I'm here! To help you get ready."

"It might be too soon in our relationship to say this, but I really love you, Liz."

About a half hour later, I was dressed in a gray sweater-dress and one high, brown leather boot. I was ready for the big dinner! Since this was the lodge's grand opening feast, they held it in the banquet hall so everyone could attend. The hall was a wide-open space filled with big round tables covered with crisp floor-length white tablecloths. Each table had a small Christmas tree in the center complete with sparkling toppers and ornaments. Roaring fires in huge hearths were on either end and large chandeliers made of intertwined elk antlers hung from the high ceilings. Green garlands adorned every shelf and windowsill, and large wreaths were hung on every wall. It felt like we were at the North Pole and Santa would come join the festivities any minute.

It took some awkward maneuvering, but Liz and Brady helped me get my wheelchair in a position where I could eat comfortably. Everyone else had just been seated too when I heard a commotion at the front of the hall not far from our table.

The whole room looked over to see the maître d' helplessly trying to stop a small but intimidating group of men from pushing their way in.

"I'm sorry, Mr. Bosley, sir, I can't let you in. This is an invitation-only event," the maître d' pleaded with the leader of the pack, a burly guy sporting a five o'clock shadow and a heavy buffalo-plaid flannel jacket.

"Where's Leach?" the man demanded, undeterred.

"This isn't the place, Dino," a frazzled-looking Archie said as he walked past my table toward the entrance.

"Oh, I think this is exactly the place, Leach. You may have convinced my parents you were looking out for Prospect's interests, but as far as I can tell, you're trying to sell our future right out from under us just to make yourself look good," spat Dino Bosley, the son of the Grand Sky Lodge's former owners. The same one Jackie had told us held a grudge against the lodge he'd once hoped to inherit.

"Dino, I know the money the pipeline people are offering you and some of the other landowners seems like a lot, but if we let this happen, we'll be selling out Prospect's entire future," Archie tried to explain. "By protecting the natural resources we've all been blessed with—"

"Easy for a fancy real estate developer to say," Dino cut in. "You're already rich."

"Now just hear me out for a minute," Archie said

firmly, standing his ground. "I've invested just about everything I have in my vision for the Grand Sky Lodge because I believe it's the right thing to do, and not just for us, but for the town. Protecting the land and stopping the pipeline is the best thing we can do for the local economy. Sure, a few individuals may gain in the short run by leasing their land, but the construction jobs they're promising will be temporary, and all the profits from the pipeline will go to fat cats at big corporations who don't care anything about Prospect or its future. They don't care if our landscape is scarred, our wildlife is killed off, or our water becomes too polluted to drink. The most valuable resource the town has is its natural beauty, not oil. Generations from now, people will still pay to visit Prospect for outdoor recreation *if* we preserve it. Otherwise there might not be anything left *to* preserve."

"Save your do-gooder act for those hippie protesters," Dino snarled.

"Gentlemen, let's talk about all this at the town hall meeting on Monday," said a mortified-looking Grant as he stepped in to play peacemaker. Only it didn't look like Dino was in a peaceful mood.

"Afraid I'm making you look bad in front of your precious guests, is that it, Mr. Conflict of Interest?" he shot back at Grant. "You're supposed to be representing the voters, and everyone I know wants this to happen."

"This is a complex issue, Dino, and there are a lot of people with legitimate concerns on both sides," Grant said diplomatically. "I'm confident that if we all work together, we can find a middle ground that everyone can—"

"Oh, middle ground, huh? You mean like going behind the town council's back and trying to turn the land we need for the pipeline into a nature preserve?" Dino shouted.

"That's Archie's idea; I haven't agreed to it," Grant protested.

I could see the wounded look on Archie's face.

"You may have some people fooled, Alexander, but you're as full of hot air as all the other politicians," Dino said, as his friends nodded and egged him on. "Me and my boys aren't leaving here until, um, until . . ."

Dino trailed off, his gaze shifting to something behind me. I turned around to see a short woman in a white chef's jacket marching down the center of the hall with an intense scowl on her face and a large, bloodstained meat cleaver in her hand. I immediately recognized her from TV.

"That's Chef Kim Crockett!" I whispered to the table.

"You. Are. Interrupting. My. Dinner," she growled in Dino's direction as she passed our table and raised the cleaver over her head.

Kim "Chef K" Crockett's triumphant run on *Top Chop Challenge* had earned her a reputation for two things in particular: a hot temper and superb knife skills.

"She's not going to . . . ," Carol started to say as Chef K pulled the cleaver back and flung it at Dino Bosley's head.

CHAPTER FIVE

A Meal to Remember

THERE WAS A COLLECTIVE GASP AS THE cleaver twisted gracefully through the air and sailed within inches of Dino's stunned head, sticking in the log beam behind him with a loud *THWACK*.

That *THWACK* got the last word. Dino and his posse instantly ran the other way without another word. Archie's and Grant's embarrassed attempts at diplomacy might not have persuaded him to leave, but Chef K's more direct approach certainly did.

"You'll all regret this!" Dino yelled from a safe distance down the hall once he was out of cleaver range.

Kim marched over to the beam, pulled out the meat cleaver, and turned back the way she'd come, throwing Archie and Grant a withering look on the way.

"I apologize for the interruption," Chef K announced to the entire hall, pausing briefly in the center of the room and glaring again at the stunned co-owners. "I promise the food is better than the security."

"Well, that was quite the appetizer," Carol remarked. "Local controversy *and* a knife-wielding celebrity chef. This is going to be the article of my career."

I bit my lip, worrying about the bad press the scene we'd just witnessed might generate for Archie and pondering what the confrontation with Dino Bosley might mean. Three things were clear: the Grand Sky Lodge's grand reopening was off to a rocky start; Dino had made my death threat suspect list; and Chef K was not to be messed with.

All of it vanished from my head as waiters began coming around to the tables with hot towels for the guests to clean their hands, signaling the start of the meal. Chef K's signature style was beautifully arranged small plates full of interesting, super-fresh local ingredients that everyone at the table could share. So instead of just one appetizer and a main course, we'd all get to try, like, ten different awesome things! I couldn't wait to see what kind of mountain-to-table delicacies she had crafted for the big opening meal.

"I can't believe I'm going to eat a meal prepared by a chef I watched on TV," I said as a waiter in a burgundy tuxedo lifted matching plush burgundy hand towels with tongs from a steaming dish and placed one on each of our plates.

"Do you think that was animal blood on the cleaver she threw at that guy, or did she chop up her sous-chef for burning the soufflé?" Carol asked, arching her eyebrows and picking up her steaming towel.

"She's got mad knife-throwing skills, that's for sure," said Brady, picking up the towel and looking at it like he wasn't sure what to do with it.

"Fancy!" Liz exclaimed, picking up her towel and then flicking it at Brady. "You wash your hands with it, doofus."

"It's like a classy moist towelette!" he replied, rubbing the towel over his hands. "Ooh, that feels good."

"You should be at the kids' banquet with Things One through Three," Liz told him.

Brady laughed. "Chicken nuggets with Santa?" I wish I were allowed in there. Brady finished washing his hands with the towel and placed it down with a shrug. "Still not totally sure why we needed those," he told us.

The towel was superhot, kind of like a sauna for your hands. Then the hot sensation lingered even after I put it down and picked up one of the appetizers the waiter had served from a separate covered dish on the same tray. I wondered if the towels had been coated in some sort of fancy essential oil.

"*Bon appétit,*" the waiter said, collecting the used towels with his tongs.

The little piece of toast with goat cheese and fresh bruschetta practically melted in my mouth.

"Oh, that's good!" I said with my mouth full. "Really good."

I could hear our housekeeper Hannah Gruen's voice

in my head telling me not to talk with my mouth full, but I just couldn't help it. It was weird, though—my hands were still oddly hot from the towel more than a minute later. Actually, they were hotter!

"Mmmmm," Brady moaned in appetizer ecstasy, gobbling down a piece of bruschetta in one bite and then licking his fingers.

"Hey, not bad!" Carol said, taking a bite.

Brady started coughing and chugged his entire glass of water in one gulp. "Oh, man, that toast thingy has some kick. My tongue is on fire."

"Mine wasn't spicy, but are anyone else's hands still hot?" Liz asked, rubbing one hand with the other. "Mine are, and I think they're turning red!"

Carol had just absently rubbed the corner of her eye. "Uh-oh," she said, squinting and quickly pulling her hand away.

Not only were my hands red, but a little cut I'd gotten on my afternoon wipeout had turned bright red and was practically throbbing. "Yeah, that kind of hurts. I wonder if—"

"Ahhhhhhh!" Carol screamed. "My eye! It really burns!"

Next thing I knew, half the banquet hall was huffing, coughing, or outright screaming! Everywhere around us people were either guzzling their water or running for the bathroom to wash their hands.

"We've been poisoned!" shrieked a woman at the table behind me.

CHAPTER SIX

~

Tropical Heat Wave

AND THEN CHAOS REALLY BROKE OUT. ALL
it took was the word "poison" to set off a chain reaction
of screams. But as I looked around the room, I noticed
that it was only the front part of the hall that was panicking. Everyone else was staring at us in confusion,
trying to figure out what was going on, including the
waitstaff as they made their way toward the back of the
hall with the trays of yet-to-be-delivered hot towels.

I looked down at my own throbbing red hands and
it hit me: there was some kind of chemical substance
on the towels!

I went to jump up to stop the waiters, only to redis-cover that I was trapped in a wheelchair with a huge cast on my leg!

"Can you tell the waiters to stop delivering the hot towels and then get Doc Sherman?" I said as calmly and quietly as I could to Liz and Brady to keep anyone else from panicking even more. "I think there's some kind of chemical on the towels that's making anything they touch burn."

Liz gave me a concerned look, then nodded. "You got it, detective."

"On it," Brady agreed, his voice hoarse from what-ever chemical he'd licked from his fingers after using the towel.

They both took off for the back of the hall.

Using my napkin, I carefully picked up a discarded towel the waiter had missed when he'd collected them and brought it slowly toward my nose. I got about as close as a couple of inches when the vapors shot up my nostrils in a peppery blast.

"ACHOO! ACHOO! ACHOO!" I sneezed

uncontrollably, a familiar hot tingle spreading through my sinuses.

It wasn't a chemical.

"Hot pepper!" I wheezed.

"Give me that," Chef K's voice demanded from behind me.

She grabbed the towel from my hand without bothering to use a napkin and inhaled deeply. I don't know how she kept from sneezing, but she barely flinched. And then she licked the towel!

"My Caribbean habaneros!" she cried.

"You can tell what . . . ACHOO! . . . kind of . . . ACHOO! . . . pepper it is?" I asked between sneezes.

"Of course I can," she shot back, as if I'd just asked Einstein if he could count to ten. "I keep twelve varieties of homegrown hot peppers hanging in the root cellar, and my Caribbean habs are the hottest, but with a complex nose combining subtle notes of tropical passion fruit and smoked cherrywood that give way to a ferocious delayed kick at the back of the palate. Some cretin walked off with an entire strand of them last week, along with a crock full of my house-fermented kraut. But how the hell did they end up on my hot towels?"

She stared at me like I might have been the one to do it, but her laser glare quickly shifted to a scrawny waiter with frizzy red hair whose name tag read CLARK.

"You!" she yelled, grabbing poor Clark by the collar like he was a bad puppy dog, nearly yanking him off his feet as he rushed past. "Tell the other waiters to stop serving the towels now and get as much milk and yogurt as you can from the kitchen to give anyone who got a hot towel."

"Milk?" Clark hesitated. "What do we need to get milk for?"

"Because if you don't, you'll be out of a job before the second course, you buffoon. Now stop asking asinine questions and do what you're told," she growled.

"Yes, ma'am," Clark squeaked, rushing off to do her bidding.

I admit her ordering milk and yogurt sounded a little weird at first, but it triggered a random lesson my high school chemistry teacher had taught us one year.

"Dairy has a compound that binds with the capsaicin oil that gives chili peppers their heat and neutralizes it, right?" I asked, the sneeze attack finally abating. "Like a hot-pepper antidote!"

She stared at me for a few moments before giving me a curt nod and stomping off. I think she was actually impressed!

Luckily, only about a quarter of the banquet hall had been "poisoned" by the habanero-spiked towels, and Chef K's milk and yogurt antidote—drunk or applied topically, depending on the victim—helped resolve the crisis so the meal could continue. I felt a little silly pouring milk over my burning hands, but it really worked! Poor Carol and her bright red, bloodshot eyes needed an eyewash from Doc Sherman, but just about everybody was back at their seats soon.

Archie and Grant were walking around personally apologizing to everyone, explaining that some harmless hot pepper had accidentally gotten sprinkled on the towels, when Chef K stomped back to the center of the room.

"We'll be sending a bottle of the lodge's finest champagne to each table to make up for the inconvenience," she announced.

I could tell by the stricken looks on both Archie's and Grant's faces that it was news to them.

"But we can't . . . ," Grant started to protest, but Chef K silenced him with one of her trademark glares.

"And," she continued, "dinner is on the house for anyone who was affected."

"That's going to cost us thousands. We can't afford this," Grant griped at Archie under his breath as they walked past.

Poor Archie. His big opening day sure wasn't going as planned. Was this latest hot pepper mishap just bad luck? Had the chili powder gotten on the towels by accident—or was it sabotage? Chef K's habaneros going missing a few days before they wound up dusted on the towels sounded like too much of a coincidence to be an accident. And the burgundy towels were perfectly colored to conceal the red pepper powder. That wasn't proof that someone planned it, but it was definitely suspicious. And if it was suspicious, it meant there might very well be a suspect. Could it have anything to do with Dino Bosley and his crew crashing the party earlier?

The questions came fast and furious, and I knew only one thing for sure: I'd just found a new mystery!

"Talk about hot towels!" George exclaimed as I eagerly filled her and Bess in over FaceTime later that evening. I was a lot less mopey than I had been when I'd called them earlier to tell them about my accident.

"I'm just glad you're okay, Nancy," Bess said sympathetically. "First you break your leg, then you're poisoned!"

"It was just hot pepper, Bess. It's not like someone put plutonium in the polenta," George said, rolling her eyes.

Georgia "George" Fayne and Bess Marvin aren't just my best friends, they're also each other's first cousins, although you wouldn't know it from listening to them.

"What I want to know is who had a motive to

sabotage that meal," I pondered, slipping easily back into detective mode. "The old owners' son, Dino Bosley, is one, but how would he manage it? Does he still have moles on the inside?"

"Sorry, Nance, sounds like a stretch to me," George said. "You want the new owners to lease a piece of land to a pipeline company, so you sprinkle hot peppers on the chef's hand towels?"

"Okay, well, speaking of the pipeline, the incident could be tied to the death threats the owners have received," I speculated. "It sounds like there are *a lot* of people in town who could be behind that, but it's going to be hard for me to do much investigating in town in this thing."

I flicked one of the wheels of my chair in frustration.

"My money's on one of the chef's kitchen staff," Bess said confidently. "It sounds like they have plenty of reason to gripe, with the way Chef K treats them."

"Meh, I'd forget about the hot-pepper angle and focus on the death threats. That sounds like the real mystery," George said. "The hand towels thing sounds like a random prank. Hey, maybe it was Bess! She's always threatening people with that pepper spray she carries around in her purse."

"Don't let her discourage you, Nancy," Bess interjected. "I think it's great you have an inside case to occupy you at the lodge while you heal."

"Seriously, I'm already going crazy from cabin fever and it's only been a few hours!" I agreed.

"And for the record, I only threaten bad people," Bess added.

"Well, I know one thing either way," George said. "A sleuth's gonna snoop, and I don't know anyone sleuthier or snoopier than our Nancy."

I'm not that *snoopy,* I thought after the call as I tried to resist the urge to peek into people's rooms with my binoculars. There were still lights on in many of the rooms, and a number of them taunted me with open curtains. I compromised with myself by agreeing to watch only public spaces.

On the mountain, the headlights from the groomers'

big snowcat machines lit up the slopes as they smoothed out the snow to get the trails ready for the morning's skiing. Out front, the lodge's grounds sparkled with Christmas lights. Even the tops of the hedges in the maze were aglow, illuminating all its geometric twists and turns as I looked down on it from the second story. A couple walked past holding hands. It was all picturesque and beautiful, but there were no clues to be found.

I nodded off in my chair, and when I woke up a couple of hours later, there were only a few rooms with lights still on. And one of them was Grant's suite— at least I assumed it was Grant's, since it was Archie who'd stormed out after their argument earlier. I didn't need my binoculars to see his silhouette walk past the window toward the door. The lights went out a moment later. I figured he'd decided to go to sleep, but a few seconds later a light went on in a room down the hall. I recognized it as a cozy little reading room I'd passed earlier. And Grant's silhouette was visible inside. So I'd learned that Grant was a night owl, but there wasn't much suspicious about late-night reading.

I yawned loudly. Grant might be a night owl, but I usually wasn't, and it had been a *long* day, full of a short but disastrous ski run, controversial pipelines, death threats, cleaver-wielding chefs, hot pepper hijinks. . . . I tried to replay it all in my mind but soon caught my chin nodding toward my chest and had to blink my eyes awake. I was so tired I'd started to fall asleep in the chair again mid-thought. It was time to retire my binoculars for the night and get some actual bed rest. I was going to wheel myself over to the bed when a dim circular light appeared at the far end of Grant's suite. His presumably *empty* suite.

I raised the binoculars to my eyes without a second thought. Suspicion confirmed! I'd used enough flash-lights in my time to recognize one when I saw one. A jolt of excitement shot down my spine as I tracked the light around the suite. The beam was too dim for me to make out the person holding it, but it sure looked like they were searching for something. Only one explana-tion came to mind for why someone would be snooping around Grant's empty suite with a flashlight.

I was witnessing a break-in!

CHAPTER SEVEN

❧

Steak Out

HOT-PEPPER HAND TOWELS WERE ONE thing, but someone breaking into an owner's suite on the night of the lodge's grand reopening? Now *that* was a real case.

The flashlight did a full sweep of the suite before retreating to the back bedroom and vanishing. I whipped the binoculars back over to the reading room door, where I'd last seen Grant step out of view. I needed to tell him!

I started to wheel myself to the door of my suite, when I caught sight of the clock.

Slow your roll, Nancy, I told myself. I'd seen what I'd seen, but I had to be sure it meant what I thought before I announced to the lodge's co-owner that I'd been spying into his room with binoculars at one thirty in the morning!

I went back over it in my head to make sure I wasn't jumping to cabin-fever-induced conclusions. Could there be another logical explanation for the flashlight appearing in Grant's suite? He wasn't traveling with anyone, and I'd seen him leave his suite and go to the reading room, so it had to be an intruder, right? I had nodded off for a minute, but surely that wouldn't have been enough time for Grant to return to the suite unseen before the flashlight appeared. Unless . . .

Could I have nodded off for longer than I thought without realizing I'd been asleep? I was pretty tired, and I hadn't looked at the clock until just now.

But even if I had, why would Grant be looking around his own suite with a flashlight instead of just turning on the lights? I'd investigated enough bizarre cases to know people do all kinds of unexpected things, but it seemed unlikely, and if there really had been a break-in, Grant and Archie needed to know. I just didn't want to announce to the world that I'd been peeping into rooms unless I knew for sure. I'd look pretty silly if I was wrong. And what if they took my binocular privileges away? I wouldn't have anything to keep me distracted while I was stuck in my room for the next six days recuperating!

The best way to avoid jumping to conclusions on a case is to get proof. All I needed to do was watch the reading room until Grant reemerged to confirm that he was still there and it really had been someone else in his suite.

I shook the cobwebs away, determined to stay awake watching the reading room all night if I had to.

So much for that plan, I thought as I woke up in my wheelchair to the sunrise coming in through my window the next morning. I had to make up for lost time. Plan B was to seek out Grant and . . . I wasn't sure about the "and" part. I still wasn't 100 percent sure he hadn't returned to his room before I saw the flashlight, and I couldn't confront him directly without letting him know I'd been snooping. Okay, so maybe Plan B wasn't the most well-thought-out plan ever. I'd just have to improvise.

As I picked up my phone, two message alerts caught my eye, and neither of them were good. The first one was from George:

CHECK UR IG. DECIDED 2 TAKE THE LODGE'S

TEMPERATURE 4 U & C WHAT PEOPLE R

SAYING . . . THE CASE OF THE HOT PEPPER

HAND TOWELS IS A HOT TOPIC!

"Ugh," I groaned as I hit the Instagram icon. Sure enough, the first post in my feed was another selfie from Carol's handle @TravelBugCarol, only this one showed her scowling with her full-on horror-movie-looking swollen, bloodshot eyes from rubbing them after using the peppered towels at dinner. The caption wasn't any better: *When a cranky celebrity chef accidentally maces her guests at a banquet catered by her "fancy" new ski resort restaurant. I cannot wait to write this article for you guys! #FineDiningFail #TravelDisaster.*

The post already had hundreds of likes. I was pretty sure this wasn't the kind of press Archie had imagined when he invited a writer from *Travel Bug* to profile the lodge.

The second text message was from my dad.

HUGE WINTER STORM IN RIVER HEIGHTS,

FLIGHTS GROUNDED FOR AT LEAST A COUPLE

OF DAYS. :(I'M SO SORRY, SWEETHEART.

CALL ME WHEN YOU GET UP.

Double ugh. We'd talked yesterday after my accident, and he was supposed to be on the first flight out this morning to keep me company while I recuperated from my broken leg. So much for that plan too.

I put the bad news out of my head. I had a break-in to investigate! Not to mention the hot-pepper towel sabotage.

I headed for the concierge's desk, figuring that was a good place to start looking. I didn't have to look far. Grant was leaning over the desk, giving hurried instructions to the man behind the desk. I did my best stealth-mode approach to see if I could overhear what he was saying.

"... I don't know how, just get maintenance up there now to change the locks anyway. My nerves are rattled enough already without having to worry about—"

CREAK, said my wheelchair. I put on my most innocent grin as Grant and the concierge turned around.

"Ah, good morning, Miss Drew!" the concierge announced. "It's wonderful to see you up and about."

My initial surprise that someone I'd never met before knew me wore off when I realized I wasn't particularly hard to spot.

"I'm Henry," he continued. "Mr. Leach told us all about your unfortunate accident. If there's anything you need, don't hesitate to let me know."

"Thanks, Henry," I replied. I turned to Grant. "Good morning, Mr. Alexander. We haven't met yet, but I'm Nancy. I did some investigation work on a case my dad handled for your firm. Archie flew me out here."

I was pretty sure my wheelchair's squeak had interrupted him telling Henry that someone had been in his suite, which gave me the perfect opportunity to confirm what I'd seen and launch my investigation into the break-in.

"Oh, yeah, Archie told me about that. Thanks," he said, sounding like his attention was still somewhere else. "Sorry about the accident. If you need anything, just ask Henry."

I could tell he was eager to walk away, but I didn't give him a chance. "I didn't mean to eavesdrop, but I overheard you say something about the lock on your door. I woke up last night and saw a suspicious light in one of the suites across from mine, so if someone was in your room, I may have seen—"

"I don't know what you're talking about," he interrupted. "My lock is fine."

"Oh, well, I thought I might have seen a flashlight in your room last night while you were out—" I began, but Grant didn't give me a chance to finish.

"You must be mistaken. I was in my room all night." He shot Henry an inscrutable look. "If you'll excuse me, I have a call to make."

He retreated hastily, leaving Henry standing there uncomfortably with a forced smile on his face. I'd just overheard Grant telling Henry to change the lock on his door. Grant was lying, but why?

"Is there, uh, anything I can do for you, Miss Drew?" Henry asked, looking at his feet.

Henry had a kind, open face, so I decided to trust him. Sometimes you just have to go with your instincts.

"Archie and Mr. Alexander told you to give me anything I need, right?" I asked.

He nodded eagerly. "Just say the word, Miss Drew."

"And Archie told you I was a detective, right?" I followed up.

"Certainly," he replied with a smile. "We've all been excited to meet you, especially me. I just love mystery novels, and I've never had a chance to meet a real live PI."

"Well, this live PI needs a CI she can trust," I said. "You know what a CI is?"

"A confidential informant!" he informed me excitedly, then looked around and lowered his voice to a whisper. *"Confidential informant."*

I grinned. I had the feeling this was going to be the start of a beautiful friendship.

"*Was* Mr. Alexander asking you about the lock on his door just now?" I asked.

"It's not just Mr. Alexander, either," Henry confidentially informed me a minute later after making me promise to keep it a secret and to help the lodge get to the bottom of whatever was going on. "You can't tell anyone I told you, but there were a few break-ins reported during the renovation and the soft launch while we were preparing to open. And not just the guest rooms; someone's been rummaging through storage rooms and supply closets too."

"Someone's been breaking into rooms and stealing things, and no one's reported it to the police?" I asked.

"That's the thing: as far as anyone can tell, nothing's been stolen," he said. "Mr. Alexander had the expensive digital SLR camera he uses to take nature photos around the grounds sitting out on the dresser, and whoever was in his room left it right where it was."

No-theft break-ins? I hadn't been expecting that.

"How did he know someone had been in his suite if nothing was taken?" I asked. "Was the lock tampered with?"

"Nope, it was locked just like he left it. He said the bed had been moved a few inches and someone had shuffled the clothes in his closet around," Henry said, lowering his voice even more. "Mr. Alexander is *very* tidy."

"Still, why not report it to the authorities so they can investigate?" I'd asked the question but realized I knew the answer before Henry gave it.

"But what if the guests find out?" He gasped. "Or Carol Fremont? It would be all over the Internet, and people wouldn't want to come!"

I nodded. Break-ins definitely weren't the kind of publicity a resort wanted, especially one with so much riding on it. And after the Instagram photo Carol had posted burning Chef K, I didn't want to see what she'd have to say about a bunch of break-ins. No wonder Grant denied that his room had been broken into.

"Some of us have been working here for years, and Mr. Leach gave us all a nice raise, too," Henry shared. "No one wants to see the lodge do poorly. We'd lose our jobs, and besides, this is like a second home for many of us. If we didn't work here, we'd have to pay for lift tickets!"

I laughed, but Henry was serious.

"Skiing is an expensive hobby," I conceded.

"What's there to report anyway? Sure, there's been a little funny business, but nothing's been taken," Henry rationalized. "No harm, no foul, right?"

"Maybe, but whoever is breaking into those rooms is after something," I told him. "And B and E is rarely done with innocent intent."

"Ooh, what do you think their motive is?" he asked excitedly.

"I don't know, Henry, but I plan to find out," I said.

I'd had the strange feeling we were being watched during our conversation, and I suddenly realized why.

"Who are they?" I asked, pointing to two huge oil portraits hanging on a nearby wall.

One was of an older man in a buffalo-plaid shirt, portly, bald, and grinning. The other was of a woman roughly the same age, but with much bolder taste. And by bold, I don't mean fashion forward. She had what's best described as a beehive hairdo, ruby-red lipstick, and the brightest blue eye shadow imaginable painted in half-moons all the way from her upper lashes to her eyebrows. Oh, and she was wearing a Hawaiian shirt.

"That's Mr. and Mrs. Bosley," Henry replied fondly. "Mrs. Bos had them commission the portraits as part of the sale agreement."

Now that he'd said it, I could see a resemblance between buffalo-plaid-clad Mr. Bosley and his son, Dino. Mrs. Bosley, though, she looked like she was one of a kind.

"She sure is, uh, flamboyant," I suggested.

"Mr. and Mrs. Bos technically ran the place together, but everyone knew Mrs. Bos was the one calling all the shots," he said.

"What's with her earrings?" I asked, noticing that her

dangling gold earrings were in the shape of a pickax in one ear and what appeared to be a mining pan in the other.

"Mrs. Bos was fond of telling guests about legends from the lodge's gold-mining days back in the 1800s," Henry recalled. "The Montana Gold Rush never amounted to much around here historically, but her grandparents told her the original owners secretly struck it rich and stashed a fortune in gold somewhere on the grounds."

Henry walked to another wall, pulled down a small frame, and brought it over.

"Her family owned the Grand Sky for the better part of the last century, and no one ever found so much as a fleck of gold dust, but she never tired of talking about it," he said. "She even made it a part of the lodge's marketing campaign when she and Mr. Bos took over running it in the 1970s."

Inside the frame was a pamphlet with a black-and-white photo of the lodge and the slogan, *Strike It Rich at the Grand Sky Lodge.*

He looked back at Mrs. Bosley's portrait. "She

insisted the artist paint her portrait in the shirt she said she was going to wear on her first day of retirement in the Caribbean. She said if she couldn't strike gold, she'd strike gold sand beaches instead."

He picked up the framed pamphlet to hang it back up, then stopped and turned around. "Actually, it's not entirely true that they didn't find *anything*. Workers did discover a hidden chamber when they tore down an old wall under the kitchen a few months ago during the renovation."

I leaned forward, anxious to hear more. "What was in it?"

"Just an empty, dusty room with an earth floor and log walls," Henry said.

"Well, that's kind of anticlimactic," I said, deflating a little.

"The contractor said it isn't unusual to find old sealed-off rooms in big historic lodges like this, but the discovery of a secret room sure gave new life to the legend for Mrs. Bos," Henry said. "She stuck around for a few weeks after the sale to see the renovation, so she was here when they found it, and she was thrilled, even if they didn't find gold."

I'd definitely found my mystery, and it wasn't kooky Mrs. Bosley and her pet legend about hidden gold. Henry did more than just confirm that Grant's room had been broken into; he'd tipped me off to multiple break-ins the lodge had been keeping under wraps. I was beginning to think the hot-pepper towels were connected too. No one was getting robbed and no one was getting seriously hurt, but the lodge certainly wasn't looking good. Could this all be about bad publicity?

I was contemplating who to talk to next when my next interview came to me. Or more accurately, she walked in my direction.

Chef K burst through the doors of the closed Mountain to Table restaurant on the other side of the lobby and stormed toward Henry. She was gripping a knife in one hand and a fistful of withered plants in the other.

"Someone is going to pay for this!" she bellowed.

~❧~

CHAPTER EIGHT

Herbicidal Maniac

"OH BOY . . . ," HENRY MUTTERED AS THE lodge's early risers turned to gawk at the chef stomping across the lobby toward the concierge desk.

"How c-c-can I help you, ch-ch-chef?" Henry stammered, looking like he'd rather run the other way.

"How am I supposed to serve poached rainbow trout with dill tzatziki and chicory flower garnish without dill and chicory flowers?!" she hollered, waving the blackened, withered plants in Henry's face.

"Um, that's a, uh, good question," Henry fumbled. "I'm not sure I'm qualified to answer—"

"Get Archie down here now," she demanded. "One of your people went into my greenhouse, turned off the heat lamps, and left the door open, and I want to know who."

Henry quickly picked up the phone and rang Archie. "Um, good morning, sir. Chef Crockett would like to see you. . . ."

Chef K leaned over the desk and yelled into the phone. "Half my herbs and seedlings are dead, which is exactly what the person who did this is going to be when I get my hands on them."

"Um, no, sir, someone seems to have gone into Chef Crockett's greenhouse without permission," Henry explained over the phone. "Yes, sir, thank you."

Henry hung up, and Archie appeared two minutes later. Archie's worry lines may have looked about ready to shriek, but he remained impressively calm as Chef K continued to rage, seemingly oblivious to me or the other staring guests.

"Are you sure someone from your staff didn't accidentally leave it open?" Archie asked when she finally took a breath.

"My people know what they're doing. I've been training most of them for years, and only a couple of them are allowed anywhere near my greenhouse," she said, looking mournfully at the dead plants in her hand. "I checked on the plants last night and closed up myself."

"I'm sorry to interrupt," I said, cautiously wheeling closer. "But I thought the lodge kept on a lot of the old staff."

Chef K snorted. "Ha! They can hire whoever they want to work in their part of the lodge, but no one sets foot in my kitchen who isn't handpicked by me, and my people know better than to mess with my babies." She shook the dead plants at Archie. "Which means it was one of yours."

"We're all on the same team here," Archie pleaded.

"Teammates don't murder people's plants!" she yelled. "This was probably the same person who stole my peppers and pulled that prank last night. I swear, if someone is trying to sabotage my restaurant—"

"Let's not jump to conclusions," Archie interrupted. "I'm sure there's an innocent explanation for all of this."

"You know what was innocent? My herbs! One more

thing goes wrong and heads are going to roll." Chef K whacked the dead plants against Henry's desk, sending wilted leaves flying as she stomped back to the restaurant.

Archie sighed deeply. "This wasn't how our first two days were supposed to go," he mumbled, massaging his worry lines.

"I'm on the case," I volunteered before he even had a chance to ask.

"Thank you, Nancy, that would be fantastic—" He hesitated. "What am I saying? I can't ask you to investigate with a broken leg! You're supposed to be resting!"

"To be honest, I'm going to go loopy without something to do," I told him. "I'm up and about anyway, and I'll keep the investigation low impact, I promise. I'll just wheel myself around and see if I notice anything suspicious."

"Why am I even considering this?" Archie asked himself. "It's a few plants, for goodness' sake. I'm sure someone just made a mistake."

"If I had to work for her, I might make a mistake like that too," Henry admitted, earning a surprised look from Archie. "What? Everyone sees how she yells at her staff. I don't know how they stand it."

"Revenge is a powerful motive," I said. "And it is a pretty big coincidence that the hot-pepper incident and the greenhouse being tampered with both happened on the same night. And with someone sneaking around br—" I halted midsentence, catching Henry nervously shaking his head behind Archie's back. Henry had trusted me with a secret, and I couldn't mention the break-ins to Archie without throwing my new CI under the bus. "I mean if someone's sneaking around behind Chef K's back, then it could be bad for business."

Archie looked like he wanted to argue but didn't have the energy. "Just keep your eyes open, that's all. I don't want you doing anything strenuous. And please don't tell anyone. It wouldn't do to have our guests or the staff asking questions and thinking something is wrong. Everyone's on edge enough as it is."

"Ooh, my first case!" Henry exclaimed as Archie sulked away. "Or my first *official* case anyway," he added with a wink when Archie was out of earshot.

"If you see anything strange, let me know. I'm going to take a ride and get the lay of the land," I told him as I wheeled myself off to explore the lodge and think.

It sure sounded like sabotage, but were the two incidents from last night really connected to the wave of un-burgled burglaries? I had the go-ahead from Archie to investigate the greenhouse massacre, so I'd focus on that to start and see if anything relevant to the break-ins turned up.

A couple of hours later and I still didn't have any more information. I wheeled myself around, did a little surveillance, and casually chatted with the staff to see if I could pick up any clues. The walkie-talkie came in handy too, since I could listen in on some of the open channels the staff used to communicate.

From what I could tell, most of Chef K's employees didn't particularly like her, but they did respect her. Sure, a lot of them were afraid of her too, but she was a great chef and she hired people who were serious about culinary art and the restaurant biz. Most of them seemed genuinely excited to learn from her and be a part of a high-profile new restaurant. They could definitely have had a nicer boss—and from everything I'd heard, she was on a real rampage after the greenhouse incident—but everything else about working at Mountain to Table sounded like a great gig, including the fact that the staff got to live on-site at a beautiful ski lodge. A harmless prank would have been one thing, but spiking guests with hot pepper and destroying important ingredients didn't seem like something a staff member would risk. Those pranks might have really harmed the restaurant. If Mountain to Table tanked, it would affect everyone who worked there, and it didn't seem to make sense for someone on the staff to sabotage their own job.

What I did know was that I was exhausted, so when Archie told me he'd take me off the case if I wasn't in bed resting by nine that night, I didn't put up a fight.

I woke up the next morning refreshed and ready to get to work. What I really wanted to do was check out the scene of the crime, but wheeling myself through the snow to the greenhouse wasn't exactly an option. There was one place I realized I could go, though, not that I was looking forward to it. I didn't think Henry would be either.

"Good morning, Nancy!" he said when he answered the phone at the front desk. "Do you have a new investigative assignment for me?"

"I actually do," I said. "Where does the kitchen keep its garbage?"

"Being a detective is less glamorous than I'd hoped," he complained an hour later while helping me rummage through bags of kitchen trash. "I can't believe this is how I'm spending my break."

"Detecting can be a dirty job," I told him.

I definitely wasn't above digging through trash in search of clues. I wasn't exactly sure what we were looking for, but if someone on the kitchen staff were to get rid of evidence, the kitchen trash might be the quickest place to ditch it without raising suspicion.

The fact that the lodge did so much composting made the job a little less gross than it could have been, since all the compostable food waste was stored in separate bins. They even had special "bokashi bins," where they used anaerobic fermentation to compost things like meat and dairy that couldn't go in a normal garden compost pile. At least we weren't elbow deep in mashed potatoes and chicken guts!

"Be careful," I said as Henry set down a bag with the telltale crash of broken dishes.

"Detecting always seems so dangerous in mystery books, but cutting myself on a broken teacup wasn't exactly what I had in mind," Henry griped, tossing aside the offending teacup, along with a bundle of dirty paper towels that had snagged on the broken porcelain.

The bundle came undone mid-toss, spilling out a pair of plastic goggles and crumpled rubber gloves.

"That's strange," I said. Rubber gloves didn't seem so weird for a kitchen; we'd excavated a few other pairs along the way and were even wearing our own. But I wondered, "Why would someone need plastic goggles?"

Henry lifted one of the gloves by its rubber fingertip.

"It looks like there's some kind of red dust on this one," he observed.

I took the glove from him, held it a few inches from my nose, and took a cautious sniff.

"ACHOO!" I sneezed.

I turned to Henry and smiled. "Looks like we found the smoking glove. Our perp must have used these to keep from contaminating themselves when they mashed up the peppers and spiked the towels."

"So it was sabotage!" he exclaimed.

"Looks like your theory about a disgruntled kitchen staffer who felt Chef K's wrath may be right," I told him.

Henry beamed with pride. "But how do we tell which disgruntled kitchen staffer? Can we take DNA samples and do a forensic test?!"

"We don't exactly have a crime lab handy," I said, but as I studied the gloves, I realized chili powder wasn't the only red thing stuck to the goggles. "Wait a second! You may actually be onto something! Although I don't think we'll need a test for this DNA sample."

Henry leaned in closer to watch as I pulled a distinctive frizzy red hair from the band of the goggles.

CHAPTER NINE

Spy vs. Spy

"CLARK!" HENRY CRIED.

I nodded, dropping the incriminating goggles into an evidence bag. "Unless there's another frizzy redhead on Chef K's staff, I'd say it's a good bet we've found our culprit. I saw her threaten to fire him last night at the banquet, and it probably wasn't the first time."

"Oh, it's not," Henry confirmed. "He's one of her favorite targets."

"If Clark stole the habaneros and spiked the towels, there's a good chance he's also responsible for killing Chef K's plants," I speculated. "Sabotaging the chef and trying to take the restaurant down with him makes more sense if he already thought he might lose his job."

"Speaking of jobs," Henry said, scrunching his nose as he tried to wipe a blob of gravy from his shirt, "I need to get changed and back to the front desk."

"Thanks for your help, Henry," I said. "I'll deliver the news to Archie."

I was wheeling my evidence bag past the large ski lounge overlooking the slopes on my way to report back on our Dumpster dive when I spotted Grant talking to someone on his cell phone. And he looked *STRESSED*. All-caps *STRESSED*. He was sitting on the far side of the lounge, facing the big floor-to-ceiling windows, and hadn't seen me, so I wheeled myself into the room as casually as I could and picked up a copy of the *Prospect Piper* daily newspaper to peek out from behind while I pretended I was lounging.

It wasn't surprising that the stories dominating the front page both involved the lodge. The headlines read GRAND SKY REOPENS TO MIXED REVIEWS and LODGE'S

THREAT TO HALT PIPELINE FUELS TENSIONS, and there was a good chance that whatever conversation had Grant so flustered had to do with one of the two topics.

Grant had a good reason not to want word of the break-in to his room to make the news and frighten guests even more. As shifty as he'd been when I asked him about it, I didn't think he'd welcome an investigation into it from me or anyone else. He might not want my help, but if I could figure out what was going on, it would help him, Archie, and the lodge.

There was no way to eavesdrop on his conversation from across the room with holiday music on the speakers and five other conversations going on, but sometimes you can learn a lot from just watching a person.

Only what I learned this time wasn't about the guy I was watching—it was about the guys watching him!

It didn't take me long to notice that I wasn't the only one peering over a periodical to spy on Grant. The blond teenager I'd seen at both the protest and Archie's speech before my ill-fated ski run hid behind a glossy snowboarding magazine. I caught sight of the brown-haired teen a moment later a few seats away on Grant's other side, lazily scrolling through his phone. At least that's what it *looked* like he was doing. He was subtle enough you'd never notice that his line of sight was aimed at Grant and not his screen—unless you'd done as much clandestine surveillance as I had.

Both guys were decked out for a day on the slopes and could easily pass as snowboarders hanging around the lounge between runs—and maybe that's what they were; there's no rule saying environmental activists can't be snowboarders, too—but unless my sleuthing senses were broken along with my leg, they were doing the same thing I was: *detecting*.

Now *that* was interesting. Why were a couple of protesters undercover, shadowing the lodge's co-owner?

I could tell Grant had no idea he was performing for an audience. The phone call appeared to get more urgent. Grant shook his head vehemently, saying no with enough emphasis that I could lip-read it before finally scrunching up his eyes like he'd just been forced to swallow some nasty medicine and then sagging in his seat. He pulled a fancy-looking gold pen from his shirt pocket and scribbled something on one of the Grand Sky Lodge courtesy notepads I'd seen lying around, then clicked off the call. He tore the note from the pad, jammed it into his pants pocket, and hurried out of the room, leaving his pen behind in his haste.

If it weren't for my broken leg, my instinct would have been to tail him, and it looked like the guys I'd seen spying on him had the same idea. I saw them exchange a quick glance, and then the blond left to follow Grant while the brown-haired one casually got up and slipped into the seat where Grant had just been. I ducked lower behind my newspaper as he gave a stealthy look around before picking up the gold pen and rubbed the tip rapidly back and forth over the center of the pad. The hint of a smile tugged at the corner of his mouth as he set the pen back down, tore the sheet from the pad, and tucked it into his pants pocket before following his friend out the door.

I gave a begrudging smile of my own—I was starting to see myself as the Grand Sky Lodge's house detective, and I didn't like the idea of someone sneaking in to spy on one of the owners—but the brown-haired undercover protester had just done the exact same thing I would have if he hadn't beaten me to it. He'd used the pen to take a rubbing of the indentation left on the pad from whatever Grant had written down. Judging from the guy's smile, it had worked, and he'd left with a do-it-yourself carbon copy of Grant's note.

Clandestinely following the guy wasn't an option, but hopefully that wasn't the only way to get in on the secret of what Grant had written on the pad before getting off the phone. I moved over to Grant's seat and picked up the gold pen (which was just as fancy up close as it looked from afar) to return it to him. After I took a rubbing of my own, of course. If I was lucky, Grant would have used enough force to leave an indentation a few pages deep.

"Darn," I muttered. With the page beneath it already ripped off, the indentation was now too faint to make out. It looked like it might be a number of some sort, but I had no way to know.

I made a mental note to find out who the boys were, thinking how busy my self-appointed house detective job was getting as I headed off to let Archie know I'd found Chef K's kitchen saboteur.

I could tell from the gasping-fish face Clark made when Archie and I confronted him in the manager's office that he was guilty. The goggles with the telltale frizzy red hair stared accusingly at him from the desk. I'd just presented him with proof that he'd spiked the hand towels with hot peppers, so I figured I'd hit him with the one-two punch. "Why did you kill Chef K's plants, Clark?"

He doubled down on his gasping-fish face and threw in a string of confused syllables to go with it. "Wha . . . I . . . uh . . . you . . . how . . . but . . . er . . . um . . . no!"

"As I see it, there are two ways we can handle this, Clark. You can have an honest conversation about what you did with Nancy and me," Archie offered. "Or I can get Chef K and leave you two alone to discuss it in private."

Clark's eyes went wide with fear. I'd have to remember to compliment Archie on his interrogation skills.

"Believe me, we're definitely the good cops in this scenario," I added.

"No! She'll kill me!" Clark blurted, images of the notoriously short-tempered chef and her ninja-like meat-cleaver skills surely dancing through his mind.

"Well, then what do you have to say for yourself?" Archie asked.

"I'm sorry," he mumbled without meeting Archie's eyes.

"Sorry?!" Archie nearly shouted, struggling to keep his clam. "I don't care how angry you are at Chef K. Your actions hurt every single person who works at this lodge."

Clark stared guiltily at his feet. "I didn't want to hurt anyone else, or even Chef, really. I was just following instructions."

"Instructions? From whom?" Archie asked incredulously. "No one who works here would have told you to sabotage our own restaurant!"

"It's true," Clark said. "I swear I never would have done it on my own."

"I demand to know who told you to do this," Archie growled.

Clark shrugged. "I dunno. I needed the money, so I didn't ask."

"Wait a second, you're saying someone paid you to sabotage the banquet?" I asked.

"Um . . . kind of," Clark said. He wasn't the clearest communicator I'd ever interrogated, that was for sure.

"But who would do such a thing?" Archie lamented.

Clark shrugged again, but I had some ideas, given the beef between the lodge and the pipeline advocates. It didn't sound like asking Clark about it would get us very far, though.

"How much did they pay you?" I asked instead, hoping he might at least be able to give a direct answer to that.

"Um, I'm not sure?" he half asked.

Archie let out an exasperated sigh.

"So someone paid you to sabotage the banquet

and Chef K's greenhouse, but you don't know who *or* how much?" I asked with a raised eyebrow. "Something's not adding up here, Clark."

"I think he's making it up to deflect blame," Archie concluded.

"No, really!" Clark insisted. "They left me notes in my room in the staff cabins, telling me what to do. I was going to say no, but they said I'd be sorry if I refused, and it was pretty creepy how the notes just showed up inside my room, so I was scared, plus the money didn't hurt, and it really wasn't my fault when you think about it. . . ."

"And you don't have any idea who could have left those notes?"

"No, I swear. They just signed them 'The Grand Sky Christmas Elf,'" Clark protested.

"And I suppose taking their money wasn't your fault either?" I asked.

"Well, I mean, I wasn't going to do it for free," he reasoned. I was getting the impression that Clark wasn't the sharpest spoon in Chef K's kitchen.

Archie looked at him like he was from another planet. "Mysteriously appearing threatening notes from elves and magical money with no denomination? Do you really expect us to believe this?"

"Uh-huh," Clark affirmed earnestly as Archie buried his face in his palms.

Clark's answers did sound ridiculous, but this was definitely supporting my theory that the break-ins and kitchen sabotage were connected. If someone really had snuck into Clark's room to leave the notes, it could be the same person who broke into Grant's suite and the other rooms. I wanted to say all this to Archie, but that would mean admitting I knew about the break-ins, and I'd promised Henry I wouldn't.

"So you don't even know how much this vanishing saboteur paid you? Did you not count it?" Archie rolled his eyes.

"Oh, uh, yeah, that's weird, isn't it?" Clark chuckled nervously.

He had been fidgeting obsessively with something in his jacket pocket. I'd initially passed it off as nerves, but every time the subject of money came up, the fidgeting got worse.

"What's in your pocket, Clark?" I asked.

"Oh, uh, that's nothing, just pocket stuff," he murmured without removing his hand.

"Pocket stuff?" I asked skeptically.

He nodded his head vigorously, willing me to believe him. "You know, like, the normal stuff."

Archie stood up. "This is absurd. I'm going to get the chef and let her deal with this."

"Wait!" Clark shouted, pulling his hand from his pocket. "I don't know how much it is because I haven't had a chance to take it to the pawnshop yet."

He reluctantly opened his hand and placed an unpolished gold nugget on the table.

~

CHAPTER TEN

Showdown at High Noon

"IS THAT WHAT I THINK IT IS?" I ASKED.

I picked up the nugget. It was about the diameter of a penny and looked like a chewed-up piece of golden bubblegum but was much heavier than I expected. And it had a distinctly visible tooth mark in it.

"I tested it," Clarke said proudly.

Gold is both heavier and softer than a lot of other metals, and one of the ways prospectors used to test whether a specimen they found was really gold was to see if biting it left an impression.

"I wonder if the rumors about people finding gold

at the lodge are true," I said, setting the nugget back down on the table in front of me.

Clark reached out to grab it back, but Archie picked it up before he had a chance.

Archie eyed the nugget carefully, then put it down just out of Clark's reach. "This is an old mining town. Little pieces of gold turn up now and again. They sell them to tourists in some of the shops on Main Street. He probably stole it from someone."

"Did not! I earned that fair and square!" Clark protested.

"I wouldn't exactly call sabotaging everyone's dinner and killing Chef K's plants fair or square," I reminded him as he slunk back down in his seat.

"I don't think I need to tell you this, but you're fired," Archie said. "You don't deserve it, but we are required to pay you for the time you worked on your final day of employment. I trust you won't go anywhere until I return with your check?"

"But what about my gold?" Clark whined.

"I think we'll display it behind the counter as part

of our decor," Archie replied, standing up and pocketing the nugget.

I wheeled myself after Archie as he left Clark behind, whimpering.

"Wonderful work, Nancy," Archie said once he'd closed the office door behind him so we could talk freely in the hall.

"Now if we can find out who gave Clark that piece of gold, we can wrap the case up for good," I replied, already mapping out the next lines of inquiry in my head. Of course, Archie didn't know that I'd be investigating the break-ins at the same time.

"Clark!" Archie scoffed. "I think one of two things is going on with Clark. Either he's off his rocker or he's pulling our leg. As far as I'm concerned, the case is closed. We found out who did it, thanks to you. I just hope it satisfies Chef K so things can go back to normal."

"I really think we should follow the investigation through and at least rule out the possibility that someone else is behind it," I argued.

"It was irresponsible of me to let you do this much," he said. "Not that I don't appreciate it. You've saved my keister twice, and I won't forget it. For now, though, I want you to rest. Doctor's orders."

"But—" I tried to protest.

"Nope," he said, holding up his hand. "Doc Sherman got wind of you rolling all over the lodge and gave me an earful. It's bad enough you broke your leg because of me. I don't want to be responsible for it not healing properly too."

Chef K marched up as we turned the corner into the lobby, with Grant following reluctantly behind.

"Where is he?" Chef K growled. She might have been the shortest of the group, but she had Archie, Grant, and me cowering.

"I think it's best for everyone if we just cut ties with him cleanly," Archie said diplomatically. "Thanks to Nancy, we know for a fact that Clark is responsible, and I've already fired him, so there's no need to—"

"Of course he's fired," she snapped. "I want him arrested!"

"Whoa, hold up a second," Grant quickly inter-jected. "The last thing we want to do is get the police involved. The important thing is we caught the person behind all this. Let's just get rid of him quietly and move on before we stir up any more bad PR."

"Oh, I'll get rid of him, all right," Chef K threatened. "I want that plant killer punished. And if you won't get the police to do it, then I'll have to do it myself."

"That won't be necessary, Chef," Archie said hast-ily as she took a determined step toward the hall lead-ing to the manager's office where unsuspecting Clark waited.

"This is a bad idea, Archie," warned Grant. "It's bad for business, and bad for us. You know what Sheriff Pruitt is like."

Chef K scowled at Archie, balling her hands into fists.

"It'll be fine, Grant," Archie reassured his partner, who looked anything but reassured. "We'll hand Clark off to a deputy and that will be it. The sooner we can be done with all this, the better."

Archie called the station, and it wasn't long before a tall officer with a gleaming, star-shaped sheriff's badge on his chest sauntered into the hotel, a deputy trailing behind him.

"Great," Grant mumbled under his breath in a way that sounded like he meant anything but.

Sheriff Pruitt had broad shoulders and a formidable potbelly. He wore a khaki uniform under a fur-collared bomber jacket with a cowboy hat on his head and a smug grin on his lips. The oversize pistol slung low on his hip made him look like he was itching for a shoot-out.

"Grant," the sheriff said, tipping his hat in Grant's direction while conspicuously ignoring Archie.

"Sheriff," Grant replied with a forced smile.

"Heard the call on the radio while I was passing by and thought I'd take this one myself," he explained. "See what was so special about this place that y'all think it's worth mortgaging the town's future."

Grant shot Archie an *I told you so* look. I remembered Jackie telling us on the ride to the lodge that

Sheriff Pruitt wasn't just pro pipeline, he was one of the people who stood to profit from it by leasing his land. No wonder Grant was worried about getting him involved.

"Let's go on back to the office, where we can talk privately," Grant suggested, clearly hoping to avoid a public scene with the police.

"Nah, I think right here's just fine," the sheriff said, giving a leisurely look around the lobby, soaking in the gaze of curious guests.

"All those poor folks in town gonna lose out on a lot of money if that pipeline has to go somewhere else," he said, shaking his head mournfully. "But I guess to some people, saving trees is more important than helping people, huh, Leach?"

"We can discuss the pipeline matter another time, Sheriff," Archie said with restraint. "Right now we have an employee who's been causing us quite a bit of trouble, and we'd like to bring a formal complaint against him."

"Funny, just realized that you're named after an animal," Sheriff Pruitt mused, ignoring him. "Is a leech an animal? Or are those slimy little bloodsuckers scientifi-cally bugs? I know you tree huggers are prickly about your science facts, and I wouldn't want to offend any-body."

Archie just gritted his teeth. I was seriously con-sidering running over the sheriff's foot with my wheel-chair for him when Chef K did us one better.

"Are you on duty?" she asked curtly.

"Excuse me?" Pruitt said, taking a surprised step back.

"Are. You. On. Duty?" she repeated one word at a time as if she were talking to someone who didn't understand English.

"It would appear so, ma'am," he replied hesitantly.

"Then save the lip flapping for the doughnut shop and do your job already," she sniped. "I didn't leave my kitchen to stand around listening to you chat."

Sheriff Pruitt cleared his throat loudly. "Now, excuse me, ma'am. Who do you think you—"

"I'll excuse you once you've completed your duties as a civil *servant*," Chef K said, emphasizing the word "servant" in a way I'm sure the sheriff didn't miss. "I think you need to work on the *civil* part of your job description, by the way. If I'm not mistaken, it's taxpayer money that pays your salary, and I'm willing to bet this resort pays more taxes to this town than just about anyone else, and that means *you* work for *us*."

Diplomacy might not be her strong suit, but she sure could get your attention.

"Now just you wait a second . . . ," Sheriff Pruitt protested.

Chef K didn't. She launched into a detailed account of Clark's crimes, from hot peppering the towels at the banquet to sabotaging the greenhouse and killing half her herbs. Sheriff Pruitt's expression turned from angry to amused as she talked, and by the time she wrapped up by demanding Clark's arrest, he was laughing so hard he was nearly in tears.

"What's so funny?" Chef K demanded. "I want that criminal arrested!"

By now the sheriff was leaning against one of the log beams with one arm and slapping his knee with the other as he tried to catch his breath from guffawing so hard.

"I just . . . Whew! . . . Give me a second here. . . . That's . . . Oh my . . . ," he said between laughs. "Now I sure am glad I took this call, 'cause that's one whopper of a tale. Hot-pepper hand towels! I gotta remember that one! Maybe try it on the deputies!"

I was glad Chef K's meat cleaver was nowhere in sight, because she was seething. "Well, are you going to arrest him?"

"Fire him if you want, but he didn't steal nothin' but a handful of habaneros, and I ain't wasting *taxpayer* money arresting a waiter for murdering some basil," he quipped, and started walking away.

He turned to Grant on his way to the door. "Talk some sense into your partner."

Archie put a gentle hand on Chef K's shoulder before she could take off after the sheriff. "I'm sorry, Chef. We can't afford to have you arrested instead."

She gnashed her teeth and stomped away in the other direction.

While the sheriff waited at the hotel door, the deputy slunk over to us with a sheet of paper. He looked rather embarrassed by the whole thing. "I'm sorry, but I'll just need you to sign the call report for our logs."

Grant reached for the pocket where his gold pen usually was, only to find it empty.

"I, uh . . . ," he said, patting his chest and then his pants pocket.

"Here you go," I said, pulling the pen from the little pouch on the side of my chair. "You left it in the lounge earlier."

"Um, thanks," he said, giving me an uncertain look as he took back the pen.

That was when I realized Grant wasn't the only one looking at me in an unusual way. The brown-haired kid from the lounge was leaning casually against the far wall, facing away from us while he played around on his phone. Actually, there wasn't anything suspicious about it at all this time—he was in a public space and he wasn't even looking at us—or there wouldn't have been anything suspicious if I hadn't used the same phony phone-scroll plus reverse-selfie-spy-cam combo move on a recent surveillance job myself. I was willing to bet he had his camera app open with the camera flipped to selfie mode so he could watch us on the screen over his shoulder without ever looking in our direction.

Gotcha, I thought, feeling every bit the Grand Sky Lodge house detective I'd imagined myself to be.

"I picked it up after the kid who was tailing you borrowed it to make a rubbing from the notepad you used during your phone call earlier today," I told Grant, pointing over his shoulder to the aforementioned stalker.

Everyone turned to look. Including Sheriff Pruitt. I'd been pretty proud of myself for spotting the guy and must have spoken louder than I'd meant to, because the sheriff heard what I said and turned to look at me. Which was basically the last thing I wanted. I had pretty quickly decided less was more when it came to Sheriff Pruitt.

"What did you say?" he demanded.

I didn't have to respond, because he could see my finger still pointing. The kid realized he'd been made, lowered his phone, and started walking in the other direction, but it was too late.

"You!" the sheriff bellowed after him. "Get over here now!"

The kid paused like he was contemplating running, but he must have thought better of it, because he turned around and walked casually back toward us. Or at least he was trying to look casual; I could see the apprehension in his eyes.

"Can I help you with something, officer?" he asked.

"I know you," the sheriff spat, grabbing him by the collar as soon as he was within reach and slamming him up against the wall face-first. "You were up front at the protest with that stupid lizard insurance sign."

"Ouch!" the kid complained.

I winced. I didn't know who the kid was or why he was spying on Grant, but I had professional respect for his spycraft and hadn't intended to get him roughed up by Pruitt.

Archie watched in shocked silence. Grant looked like he wanted to crawl into a hole somewhere and disappear.

Pruitt frisked him roughly, pulling a Swiss Army knife and a phone from the kid's pockets and tossing them both on the floor, before getting to his wallet.

"Hey! You don't have probable cause to search me! I haven't done anything illegal!" the kid protested.

"Spying on a state representative gives me all the cause I need," Pruitt replied, twisting the kid's arm behind his back.

"Ow!" he yelped.

"You're hurting him!" Archie cried.

"Sheriff, this isn't necessary," said Grant, trying to intervene.

The sheriff shot him a withering look. "It wouldn't be if you watched your own back."

Pruitt pulled out the kid's driver's license.

"Frank Hardy from Bayport," he read. "Where the heck is that?"

He tossed the license over his shoulder and started flipping through the billfold.

Frank Hardy, I thought. *I know that name.* While I was searching my memory banks to figure out from where, Sheriff Pruitt pulled a folded piece of paper from Frank Hardy's wallet. I could see the Grand Sky Lodge letterhead and the edge of the ink rubbing as soon as he opened it.

The sheriff read it silently to himself, clenching his jaw tighter as he did, then stuffed it in his own shirt pocket. This definitely wasn't going how I'd envisioned.

Pruitt turned to Grant, his expression deadly serious. "You told me yesterday you thought somebody broke into your suite?"

Grant nodded sheepishly, avoiding looking at either me or Archie.

"You didn't tell me that!" Archie exclaimed.

So he *had* reported it to the police. Or to Sheriff Pruitt, at least. But why would he hide it from Archie?

"I saw a flashlight go on in Representative Alexander's suite late the night before last, but it was too dark to tell . . . ," I started to fill them in, but Pruitt didn't wait for me to finish. He yanked the Hardy kid's arms behind his back instead.

"Frank Hardy," he snarled, pulling out his handcuffs, "you are under arrest for breaking and entering."

"Hey! You can't—" both Frank Hardy and I started to shout at the same time as Sheriff Pruitt slapped the cuffs on his wrists and yanked them tight.

"Ow!" Frank screamed.

"I've got the little lady in the hot rod as my witness," said Pruitt, nodding in my direction.

I didn't know what I was madder at, him misstating what I'd said or calling me little lady!

"I didn't witness any such thing," I objected. "In fact—"

"You can give a statement later," he cut me off, shoving Frank in front of him toward the door.

"Hey, Sheriff," the deputy said, holding up the tweezers from the Swiss Army knife. There was a visible crease in one of the prongs, where it had been bent. "Check this out."

The deputy was able to easily bend the creased

prong to a ninety-degree angle. Then he pulled out the plastic toothpick, which was gnawed up one side like it had been rubbed back and forth over something metal. Archie and Grant both looked at the deputy in confusion.

"You can use the bent tweezers and toothpick from a Swiss Army knife as a DIY lock pick," I clued them in, recognizing instantly what the deputy meant.

"Been using these to pick your nose, Hardy?" the sheriff asked, giving him a shove.

Okay, that was suspicious. It was only circumstantial evidence, though.

"There's nothing illegal about having bent tweezers!" Hardy argued. "It isn't proof of anything!"

"He's right," I agreed. "It's a little suspicious, sure, but—"

"Did I ask you, Hot Rod?" the sheriff said, cutting me off again. *Argh*, that was getting really annoying.

"This is a wrongful arrest in violation of the Fourth Amendment pursuant to Title 42, section 1983, of the US code!"

Frank Hardy and I exchanged a surprised look. We'd both quoted the same law at the same exact time!

Pruitt glared daggers at both of us. "I'm not about to let a burglar and a little girl tell me how to do my job."

I bristled at the sheriff's obnoxious barb, but any question I'd had about whether Frank Hardy was a fellow detective vanished. I still wasn't sure whether he was one of the good ones or the bad ones—and the world definitely has both—but I knew he didn't deserve to be arrested. *Yet.* The kid and his partner could very well have done it, but even if they had . . .

"I'm sorry, Sheriff, but this little girl knows enough about law enforcement to tell you that you don't have enough evidence to make a legal arrest," I shot back.

"If Frank Hardy here doesn't like it, he can talk to the judge about it at the bail hearing," Sheriff Pruitt replied. "Next week, when Judge Simers gets back from his Christmas vacation."

CHAPTER ELEVEN

The Dream Team

"WHAT JUST HAPPENED HERE?" ARCHIE asked, looking from me to Grant as Sheriff Pruitt pushed Frank Hardy out the front door. "Why didn't you tell me your suite was broken into?"

Grant looked away. "I'm sorry, Arch. I didn't want to worry you any more than you already are."

"And why was that poor kid following you?" Archie asked.

Grant just shook his head and shrugged.

"Hopefully that oaf Pruitt is right about that boy and this puts an end to the break-ins and everything else."

Archie sighed deeply and looked back at me. "I know your intentions are good, Nancy, but please, no more investigating. You need rest, and our problems are our concern."

Archie trudged back toward the manager's office, where Clark was still waiting. Grant quickly walked in the other direction before I could ask him what the note said.

Archie had asked what happened, and to be honest, I wasn't entirely sure. It had hit me where I knew the name Frank Hardy from, though. He was one of the "Hardy Boys," a pair of teen brothers from somewhere on the East Coast who'd made a name for themselves as amateur PIs. The under-twenty-one gumshoe crowd isn't exactly a crowd, so I tend to notice when I hear about others with my unique hobby. I'd read a magazine feature on them called "A Con Artist in Paris," about an international art case they'd cracked not too long ago. I think Frank was the older one, and thanks to me, he was about to spend Christmas in jail, whether he deserved it or not.

The younger brother was named Joe, and he was

headed right toward me with a very unhappy look on his face.

"I was shooting the whole thing, so whatever it is you're trying to cover up by having my brother arrested isn't going to work," the blond kid from the lounge spat, holding up his phone. "That was a bogus collar, and you know it."

A video? Talk about bad publicity. At least Carol wasn't there to see it. It might not look good for the lodge if video of a police bust went online, but, even if it did, I was still okay with it.

"I'm glad you documented it," I said, catching him off guard. "Law enforcement's duty to protect and serve is one of the most important responsibilities in a democratic society, and officers should be held accountable when they abuse their power or violate a person's rights."

"I, uh . . . exactly," he said, clearly confused that I'd agreed with him.

"Even when that person may have broken the law," I continued.

"Hey! Wait a second! Frank didn't break any laws!"

he shouted. "That B and E charge is totally bogus!"

"And the DIY Swiss Army lock pick Frank was carrying?" I asked.

"A bent pair of tweezers doesn't prove anything, and if you were good enough to make our tail, then you have enough experience sneaking around yourself to know it," Joe argued. "I'm not going to fib and say Frank and I have never had to pick a lock on a case before, but those tweezers haven't been used for anything but tweezing for years."

I couldn't argue with that. I'd opened a door or two I maybe wasn't supposed to while investigating, and I definitely wasn't a burglar.

"Then why were you tailing Grant Alexander?" I asked.

"Why are you working for Grant Alexander and the pipeline people?" he demanded in response.

"I'm working for Archie Leach and the lodge, not . . ." I paused as the last part of his question sank in. "What do you mean, Grant Alexander *and* the pipeline people?"

He eyed me for a moment before answering. "The pipeline's not paying your tab?"

"I don't have a tab. You could say I'm the unofficial house detective," I told him. "And I've never even met anyone from the pipeline."

"Don't be so sure of that. Why do you think we were tailing Alexander?" he asked.

"That's ridiculous," I said. "He's the co-owner of the eco resort that's standing in the pipeline's way. It just doesn't make sense. I know there are some political land mines he has to navigate, but a business relationship with the pipeline would be a huge conflict of interest. Archie would never let that happen!"

"You mean conflicts of interest like secret meetings with pipeline honcho Larry Thorwald?" Joe asked smugly.

"It's not that strange for a politician to meet with executives of a high-profile project like this," I suggested.

"Why sneak around and hide it, then? And what about the links we found between subsidiaries of the pipeline's holding company and the representative's campaign manager?" Joe prodded. "*And* the note Sheriff Poo-it stole had a phone number with the same area code as Thorwald's."

"Did you recognize the number?" I asked after I stopped laughing at Sheriff Pruitt's new nickname. Maybe I was going to find out what Grant wrote on that note after all.

"I didn't see it." Joe looked as disappointed as I did. "Frank just told me it was a number with the same area code and the initials *TS*. Does that mean anything to you?"

I racked my brain for a minute. "Nobody here with those initials that I know of. Who hired you on this case, anyway?"

"No one. We hired ourselves," he said.

That sounds familiar, I thought. Archie may have given me the okay to investigate Chef K's saboteur, but I had taken the break-in case on my own and dubbed myself the Grand Sky Lodge "house detective" without actually telling the people I was detecting for.

"We flew in with the Bayport High Green Environment Conservation Club to join the pipeline protest, and figured the best talent we brought to the cause was our detecting," he explained.

Green Environment Conservation Club? Well, that solved the mystery of the odd GECCOS sign they'd been holding at the protest.

"So we started digging into the pipeline's finances to see if we could turn up anything shady that might help bring the project to a stop," Joe continued.

"And that led you to Representative Alexander?" I asked.

Joe nodded. "Enough links that it's definitely suspicious."

"Anything illegal?" I asked skeptically. I didn't want to believe Grant could be working to undermine his own business. "Don't forget, he's a victim in this too. I saw someone break into his suite with my own eyes."

He looked stumped by that.

"Nothing outright illegal *yet*, but there's definitely

a conflict of interest and maybe a lot worse. Something smells fishy, and where there's smoke, there's usually smoked fish," he declared confidently.

"Um, I hope your detecting is stronger than your metaphors," I said.

I knew one thing for certain, though: even if Frank or Joe *had* been involved in the break-in—and my detective instincts were telling me I could trust Joe—Frank's arrest was *definitely* illegal and more than a little fishy in its own right.

"Stopping the pipeline is a worthy cause, and I want to do whatever I can to help Archie and the Grand Sky Lodge succeed," I said. "I'm not convinced you're right about Grant, but there's definitely something smoked fishy going on, and I'm going to help you and your brother find out what. Right after we get Frank out of jail."

"I hope your detecting is better than your skiing." He held out his hand, grinning at my enormous cast. "I'm Joe."

"It's much better!" I laughed and shook his hand. "I'm Nancy. Nancy Drew."

"Hey, I've heard about you!" he exclaimed.

"And I've heard about the Hardy Boys," I replied. "Looks like the world's top teenage detectives are about to team up to solve a case."

CHAPTER TWELVE

Fire and Funk

ONE OF THE FIRST THINGS JOE AND I DID was call our dads to try and get Frank out of jail. One of the perks of having a prominent legal eagle as a father is being able to call on him to solve problems like this one. He might be stuck all the way back in River Heights because of the snowstorm, but he'd just found his next client right here in Prospect, Montana.

And it turned out Joe and Frank's dad, Fenton Hardy, was a famous detective with his own set of law enforcement strings he could pull to help Frank out. It wasn't just Nancy Drew and the Hardy Boys teaming up; it was also our dads, in a double family team-up! Between Carson Drew and Fenton Hardy, we were hoping Sheriff Poo-it was going to be having a very bad day.

I had a strong hunch I could trust Frank and Joe, so I believed Joe when he said that they had nothing to do with the break-ins. But even if I turned out to be wrong, the arrest had still been illegal. Due process exists for a reason, and I'd rather see a guilty person get to exercise their rights and be convicted justly than an innocent person wrongly imprisoned. If the police got to push around and arrest anyone they wanted without probable cause or sufficient evidence, we wouldn't have a democracy. If Frank was guilty, I trusted myself to prove it during my investigation and bring him to justice, but not without proof. And definitely not with excessive force.

Speaking of suspects, the last thing I asked Joe before we parted ways was what he knew about hot-pepper hand towels and herbicide. He looked at me like I was from outer space, and unless he was a better actor than I was a detective, his reaction was sincere. He didn't know anything about either incident. If someone had paid Clark a golden nugget to sabotage the banquet and Chef K's greenhouse like he'd claimed, I was pretty sure it wasn't Frank. The sabotage might still be related to the pipeline, but Joe and Frank hadn't stumbled on the connection yet if it was.

It can be hard to admit when you're wrong, but I definitely regretted calling out Frank in front of the sheriff. I took the case against myself to Archie, who didn't exactly look happy to see me.

"I appreciate your concern, Nancy, but I think cabin fever may be getting the best of you," Archie said after I finished. "You've caught *two* suspects, and that's more than enough for one vacation. What you need now is *rest*. The case is closed, thank goodness. From here on, the week should be smooth skiing!"

I tried to protest but just got more of the same. Sometimes people want so badly to believe things are okay, they'll trick themselves into thinking they are even when they really aren't—even if it means ignoring facts. I was going to have to continue my investigation on the DL for the moment. Archie might not see it now, but it was for the lodge's own good. There was a big chance that whoever hired Clark was still out there, and I was the only person trying to find them.

Conducting an investigation from a wheelchair while pretending not to conduct an investigation is hard work, and I didn't make much progress until that evening. Although I'm not sure "progress" is really the right word.

With my stomach rumbling, I headed for Mountain to Table to meet Carol for the first dinner seating of the night and resume my covert surveillance of Chef K's staff.

Unfortunately, it didn't take much surveilling to see the decorative Hanukkah menorah in the restaurant's entrance erupt into flames.

Carol had her phone out in an instant and was recording with glee as the maître d' rushed to put the fire out with the fire extinguisher. Talk about a festival of lights! Luckily, these flames didn't last eight days. They did incinerate the drapes and fill the restaurant with smoke, though.

The "candles" on the menorah were made of plastic with electric bulbs shaped like flames, but it was a very real fire that erupted from them and set the drapes alight. And from the smell that lingered after the extinguisher had safely doused the flames, I knew exactly why.

Butane, I thought.

The only reason you'd smell lighter fluid coming from an electric menorah was if someone had tampered with it. The restaurant had just reopened after closing between the lunch and dinner shifts, giving someone time to meddle while no one was around. It was brilliant in a way, because everyone would think it was yet another accidental mishap in Chef K's short run at Grand Sky Lodge. And I was starting to think the saboteur might want to keep it as short as possible.

I'd have to take that info to Archie. He wouldn't

want to hear it, but I was pretty certain the sabotage hadn't stopped with Clark's dismissal.

"Oh, this is pure social media gold," Carol cooed as she posted the video to Instagram.

Gold! If only she knew. It looked to me like Clark's nugget-dropping benefactor was still in play.

"Honestly, Nancy, I think you're being paranoid. Sometimes an accident is just an accident," Archie said dismissively later that night after taking an uncomfortable minute to process my theory about the spontaneously combusting menorah. "I think you're just feeling guilty about that Hardy boy who broke into Grant's suite being mistreated by the police. And I don't blame you; the way Sheriff Pruitt pushed him around was shameful, but that doesn't mean he isn't guilty."

I knew right away arguing wasn't going to get me anywhere. I was going to have to give him enough evidence that he believed it for himself. You know that thing I mentioned where people want so badly to believe something that isn't true that they convince themselves that facts aren't really facts? I learned on a case that there's actually a psychological term for it: cognitive dissonance. That basically means the discomfort people feel when something proves the thing they want to believe is wrong. My dad likes to say, *Just because someone tells you something you don't want to hear doesn't mean it isn't true.* I figured they were pretty good words to live by, but I had a hunch Archie definitely wouldn't want to hear them.

That changed the next day when half the lodge woke up to the smell of rotten sauerkraut.

"What is that smell?" I asked the empty room as the odiferous funk of warm fermented cabbage assaulted my nostrils, pulling me out of a perfectly pleasant holiday dream about riding around the grounds in a one-horse open sleigh.

I opened my eyes to find that my room smelled terrible. It smelled like hot, spoiled cabbage. Talk about a rude awakening.

It was clear I wasn't the first person to call Henry to

complain about it. Every room on my side of the lodge and Mountain to Table's dining room was filled with the same funky smell. It didn't take long for the maintenance crew to find the crock of kraut inside the heating system, placed just so to deliver fermented air un-freshener into our rooms along with the heat. It also didn't take long for Chef K to confirm that the crock in the vents was indeed the same one that Clark had pilfered along with the habaneros he used to spike the towels at the banquet.

Guests were starting to check out, Carol was lighting up social media with pictures and posts about all the mishaps, and Chef K was on a full-steam-ahead cranky-chef rampage. She was obviously used to being the one doing the terrorizing, not being terrorized. She wasn't the only one affected by the hot-pepper hand towels and fermented cabbage stink bomb, but causing mayhem for her and the restaurant certainly seemed like the prime objective of every mishap that had happened so far. What I didn't know was who was behind it all—or why.

Archie had to concede that a stolen fermentation crock full of rotten sauerkraut hadn't dropped into the heating ducts by accident. Somebody had put it there. And with Archie's hopes of smooth skiing thrown stinkingly off course, he finally agreed to let me find out who the stinker was.

"We have too much riding on this week not to," he admitted.

Nobody's week was going as planned. When I finished talking to Archie later that morning, there was a voice mail waiting for me from my dad. His travel prospects weren't looking good. River Heights and the rest of the Midwest were getting slammed by *another* winter storm. Holiday air travel was a mess everywhere, and he might not be able to make it at *all*.

I tried to put my disappointment aside and focus on the case.

Now that my investigation was official, I tracked down Chef K for an interview as Mountain to Table prepared to open for brunch.

It didn't go well. She denied having any enemies

who would want to sabotage her or the restaurant and then promptly kicked me out when I gently suggested it might be another disgruntled employee like Clark who she hadn't been nice to. I could hear her yelling at her sous-chef as I left.

The maître d' apologized and suggested I come back later when she might be in a better mood. I thanked him for the suggestion, but I didn't think another interview would get me anywhere.

Chef K was being unhelpful to her own detriment. Her restaurant was suffering the most from all these so-called pranks. In fact, with the exception of the hotel break-ins, everything that had gone wrong had happened in her dining room, with materials she created or had access to. Could she be the one doing the sabotaging? Was she intentionally trying to frustrate my investigation to cover her tracks, or was she really that surly?

I had just picked up my phone to make a call when it buzzed preemptively in my hand.

"Joe!" I said as I answered. "Great detectives think alike. I was just about to call you."

"Frank is free!" Joe cheered over the phone. "Operation Hardy-Drew Dads had Poo-it so scared of a wrongful arrest lawsuit that Frank said he was quaking in his cowboy hat when he let him go."

"Score one for the good guys! At least I hope you guys are the good guys," I (mostly) joked.

"Har-har, Drew, very funny," Joe said, but I could tell he was smiling. "The bad news is, Frank has been banned from the Grand Sky, so I'll be flying solo for any investigating you need help with at the lodge."

That was frustrating, but not surprising. I had caught Frank spying on one of the owners, after all.

"And," Joe continued, "Poo-it conveniently *lost* the note with the number Alexander wrote down, and Frank didn't happen to memorize it before the sheriff took the note from his wallet. So all we have to go on are still the initials *TS* and the fact that we know *TS* has the same area code as Thorwald."

"Ugh," I grumbled. "What's your next move?"

"Well, Frank's cover's been blown, thanks to someone we know," he jabbed.

"Sorry," I mumbled.

"So I'm going to keep a tail on Thorwald, and Frank is going to work his nerd magic on the computer to see what else he can find out about the pipeline's financial connections to Representative Alexander and his campaign," he said. "And trust me, no one has nerdier magic than my big bro."

"Oh, is that so?" I asked, a grin creeping across my face. "I think my friend George may have something to say about that."

I explained that George was definitely the best when it came to online research and general investigative technology geekery, but he didn't want to hear it.

"Oh, it's so on, Drew," he said. "Well, George is going down. Frank is going to crush her."

"Who am I going to crush?" I heard Frank ask in the background.

"Yes!" George shouted over the phone a few minutes later when I filled her in on the challenge. "I love a good hack-off!"

I caught her up on the details of the case to launch

her search and gave her the twenty-four-hour "hack-off" deadline Joe and I had agreed to.

"Looks like I've already got a head start on that Hardy amateur," she said gleefully. "All those negative posts that travel writer Carol Fremont has been making inspired me to do a little digging. Turns out, before she got the cushy gig at *Travel Bug*, she was an independent travel blogger."

"Um, sounds like a pretty normal career path for a travel writer to me," I commented.

"Yeah, but it was what she blogged about that caught my eye," George insisted. "She made her name writing hit pieces that slammed travel destinations any time something went wrong. The blogs are funny and stylish, but they're also totally sensational and downright vicious some of the time. And they got her a *ton* of hits to help launch her pro writing career."

"Not too surprising, really, seeing how eager she is to tell everyone on social media as soon as something goes wrong," I said. I liked Carol, but the joy she seemed to get from others' misfortune wasn't her best personality trait.

"Well, things seem to go wrong *a lot* when Carol Fremont checks into a place," George said, adding the next piece to the puzzle. "Fires, burst pipes, food poisoning, theft, even snakes. It's almost uncanny. Everywhere she went for a couple years before she landed the *Travel Bug* gig was some kind of crazy vacation disaster, and each one got her more followers and boosted her profile."

"You're saying you think she *makes* things go wrong just so she can write sensational stories about them?" I asked.

"I don't know, but bad luck has been pretty darn lucky for her, and she seems to get a lot luckier than your average vacationer," George said. "The online content world is supercompetitive, and people can be pretty cutthroat when it comes to getting ahead."

"Oh, she's definitely competitive," I informed George. "She's totally determined to land the *Travel Bug* cover with this story."

"It would be her first one," George told me. "She's written a bunch of articles for *Travel Bug*, but none of them have made a big enough splash to make the cover. So the question is—"

"Is she competitive enough to manufacture the travel hit piece to end all travel hit pieces in order to make it happen?" I finished George's thought for her.

The implication gave me chills. Would someone really go to such extreme lengths to boost their own career? I'd seen on other cases how competition and greed could drive a person to do some pretty crazy things, so I knew the answer was yes. But was Carol someone like that?

Her social media posts lambasting the lodge to promote her article were getting a ton of hits for both her and the magazine. I didn't know if she would stoop to that level, but she was definitely benefiting from it.

"I'll keep an eye on her," I said.

Only it turned out to be someone else I found my eye on next.

Later that night, after staring at the backs of my

eyelids for a few hours as my mind raced through all of the case's peculiar complexities, I decided to give up the ghost on a good night's sleep and pick up my binoculars. It was already after midnight, and the lodge was pretty quiet, with lights on in only a few rooms. Carol's room and Grant's suite were both dark, and the grounds were perfectly still. And beautiful! With the day's fresh snowfall and the holiday lights sparkling, it looked like a Christmas dream.

The peaceful scene had just about lulled me to sleep in my chair when movement off to the side of the lodge brought motion to the still life and shook me awake. A figure was making its way through the snow beyond the shoveled paths toward the shadows at the edge of the lodge.

I raised the binoculars to my eyes, adjusting the focus to bring the person into sharp relief. Whoever it was looked bundled up against the cold, with a scarf covering the lower half of their face, but the determined look in the person's exposed eyes made it easy for me to identify her.

What was Chef K doing trudging through the snow at the witching hour?

She looked furtively over her shoulder, like someone might be following. Then she vanished behind the lodge, moonlight glinting off the knife in her gloved hand.

CHAPTER THIRTEEN

~

Hunted

THE FIRST THING I DID THE NEXT MORNING was call Liz and Brady. I planned to investigate Chef K's midnight wanderings, and I was going to need some help.

I'd stayed up for hours, hoping to glimpse Chef K returning—and hopefully without a bloodstained knife!—but she never reappeared. Which was odd, because there weren't any entrances that I knew of on that side of the lodge. What was odder was the knife. Who takes a hike through the snow at midnight carrying a deadly weapon? Unless they plan to use it.

The knife had been about four inches long with a wicked curved blade that almost looked like a mini scythe. I shivered as the image of Chef K as a culinary grim reaper popped into my head. I had no idea why she'd ventured out in the middle of the night armed with a knife, but the possibility that she wanted to catch the culprit on her own and exact revenge definitely flashed through my mind.

What *was* Chef K hiding? I wondered if there was a reason someone was targeting her kitchen that she didn't want us to know about. Hopefully, following this lead would be the breakthrough I needed to solve the case.

I didn't know what we were facing. Liz said she would sign Things One through Three up for ski school that day. We all agreed that this wasn't a mission for kids.

It wasn't a mission for me, either, not without some professional help, at least. My old-fashioned wheelchair wasn't exactly built for following a person's tracks through the snow. But that didn't mean it couldn't be modified.

"Cross-country skis," Liz said definitively. "We'll turn your wheelchair into a chariot, and Brady can pull it like a horse!"

"An especially handsome horse," he added.

"As fancy as a chariot pulled by Brady sounds, wouldn't it still be easier to just push me?" I asked.

"Yeah, I guess," Liz conceded. "Way to ruin all the fun, though."

A quick call to Henry at the front desk, who made a quick call of his own to the rental shop, earned us a pair of cross-country skis that met Liz's specifications, and with a bit of tinkering, Liz and Brady had them strapped under my wheels in no time. My wheelchair had been transformed into a ski-chair!

"I trained with some amazing Paralympic skiers after my crash who inspired me never to give up," Liz shared. "They used all kinds of great adaptive gear that allowed them to ski with their different abilities and go anywhere on a mountain they wanted, and now you can too!"

"That's really cool, but I still think I'll leave the

double diamonds to you," I told her. "I'm definitely down for some deep-snow detecting, though!"

It hadn't snowed since yesterday and there hadn't been much wind overnight, so the conditions were perfect for tracking. Chef K's boot prints stood out in clear relief in the snow. Brady wore snowshoes to make pushing my ski-chair easier, while Liz skied alongside me on a pair of her own cross-country skis.

"She couldn't have been walking far in this stuff without snowshoes," Liz observed.

"Tell me about it!" Brady huffed. "Chariot pushing is a workout even with snowshoes."

"I think you're right, Liz. The tracks look like they lead behind that shed." I pointed to one of the small wooden outbuildings off to the side of the lodge.

My heart began to beat faster. What were we going to find?

"Well, it's definitely not a body," Liz remarked, looking at the disturbed snow behind the shed.

"What is it, though?" I asked as Brady pushed me

closer to what looked like frost-covered glass window-panes buried in the snow.

"A trapdoor!" Brady exclaimed, eagerly reaching down to open it.

"Careful," I cautioned. "We don't know what's inside."

This was it! A clue so important that Chef K felt the need to hide it in a trapdoor buried in the snow. I was buzzing with anticipation as Brady carefully lifted the first windowpane to reveal its secrets.

"Is that kale?" Liz asked.

"Ooh, and Swiss chard, I think, too," Brady said, snapping off a large red leaf and taking a bite. "Yup! These clues taste great!"

We'd found a clue, all right. The clue to growing cold-hardy greens like kale, chard, and spinach out-doors in the winter! The windowpanes covered wooden boxes about two feet deep with lush foliage growing inside. Once the boxes were open, I recognized them immediately.

I blushed with embarrassment at my big "clue."

"They're called cold frames. Our housekeeper Hannah tried using them one year to extend the garden's growing season. The glass acts like a mini greenhouse, warming up the soil enough for frost-tolerant veggies to keep growing even in the snow."

I looked at the freshly severed stems on three of the plants. "It looks like the only thing Chef K got revenge on last night was the kale. I'm pretty sure that wicked-looked curved blade she had was just a pruning knife. Hannah keeps a smaller one that looks kind of like it in her garden bag."

I hung my head. My first trip outside the lodge since breaking my leg had led to a dead end.

"Well, where'd she go from here?" Liz asked, undeterred. "You'd said she went behind the lodge and didn't come back. Maybe there's still more to the mystery."

"You're right!" I agreed, perking up instantly. What was I pouting about? A good detective has to be persistent, and I wasn't about to let either a broken leg *or* salad greens get me down. "Onward, driver! Follow those tracks!"

They might not lead to the huge revelation I'd hoped, but I was outdoors with friends and I was at least going to have some fun!

"That's strange," I muttered a couple of minutes later as we followed the tracks around the side of the lodge right into another dead end. And by dead end, I mean the boot prints led straight into one of the lodge's solid log walls!

"Where'd she go?" Brady wondered, as the three of us looked at the tightly interlinked logs of the lodge's old log-cabin-style exterior. There weren't even any windows. We were on the side of the lodge where the restaurant was, but there was no way for anyone to get inside. Did Chef K have secret Spider-Woman powers?

"It's like she just vanished," Liz said, sliding closer to the wall. "Maybe she's a ghost!"

"The ghost of Christmas dinner!" Brady joked.

There was a muffled click as Liz reached forward with her left ski pole to slide herself closer to the wall. "What was . . . ?"

The question was cut off by a loud metallic *SNAP*

as a pair of metal jaws leaped from the snow and slammed shut on the bottom of her ski pole, snapping it clean in half.

Liz jumped. I gasped. Brady screamed like he'd been the one to trigger the trap and rushed over to her.

"I'm okay, sweetie," she reassured him, eyeing the metal trap now lying in the snow with the clipped-off end of her ski pole in its jaws. "Angry, but okay." She scowled as she leaned down to pick up the antique iron trap. "It's just my stupid pole, but if I hadn't been wearing skis, I could have stepped right on it. If it had been someone in boots or snowshoes, they could have been really hurt."

The jaws were two rusty iron bands clamped together like a pair of angry metal lips with a heavy chain hanging off them. There was an iron plate underneath that must have triggered it when Liz unwittingly poked it with her ski pole.

"It's an old animal trap like the ones hanging on the wall in the lodge from when trappers used to stay here during the fur trade era," I observed, my heart still racing as Liz held up the trap so I could examine it. "Only I'm guessing this one wasn't meant for animals. It looks like someone filed down the teeth, so it wouldn't actually impale anyone."

"Well, that was nice of them," Liz said sarcastically.

I looked from the lighter-colored filed iron edges where the teeth had been to the century-old rust covering the rest of it. Whoever had done the filing, it had been recent.

"It's like they were trying to scare someone, not necessarily trap them." I shuddered as I watched Liz strain to reopen the jaws of the heavy iron trap. Even without the metal teeth, stepping in it still could have broken someone's foot.

"I'd like to trap someone right about now," Liz growled, jabbing the air with her broken pole. "This is the nastiest prank yet."

"The question is, who was it meant for?" I wondered aloud.

Chef K's boot prints stopped just a foot to the right of the trap, and there was no way to tell whether she'd known to avoid it or had just gotten luckier than Liz and missed it.

"Do you think Chef Angry Apron left it as a booby trap in case someone followed her—or do you think it was meant for her?" Liz's scowl turned to confusion as she looked from the trap to lodge wall. "And where the heck did she go, anyway?"

"This is freaking me out, guys," Brady whispered, speaking up for the first time. "Let's get out of—"

Brady's sentence was cut off by a loud, creaky moan that sounded like two ancient tree trunks rubbing together from inside the wall. Liz raised her broken ski pole like it was a weapon, Brady whimpered, and I just stared as a huge hidden door cracked open in the side of the lodge.

CHAPTER FOURTEEN

~∞~

Open Sesame

STANDING ON THE OTHER SIDE WITH AN intense scowl and a meat cleaver was Chef K. The hidden door certainly explained how she'd gotten back inside the lodge, but I was suddenly less concerned with that than what she planned to do with the cleaver.

"What in the world is going on out here?" she snarled before cutting herself off with a gasp when she saw the animal trap lying in the snow in front of her secret door, its metal jaws still clinging to the tip of Liz's ski pole. From the way the color drained from

Chef K's face, the answer to Liz's question from a moment earlier was obvious. The trap had been set to catch her.

"What—what—what is that?" she stammered, looking at the trap.

It was the first time I'd seen Chef K look the least bit rattled. Angry, oh yeah. Loud, definitely. Just never unsure of herself before now. Even when half the banquet hall was screaming from being hot peppered, she'd come off as confident and in command. But the trap had her shaken.

"It's definitely not a welcome mat," Liz quipped. "Nice secret door, by the way."

"But no one knows about this entrance!" Chef K insisted.

"Tell that to whoever put the trap there," Brady said.

"If we were able to track you here, someone else could have as well," I told her.

"Who is behind all this stuff? Why are they doing this?" she whispered, sounding downright vulnerable.

"Can we come in?" I asked. "I plan to find out, and it's probably best that they don't see us talking."

She stepped aside without answering and let Brady push my ski-chair inside, with Liz following close behind.

She swung the secret door closed behind us. The heavy door groaned, then locked into place with a *THUMP*. It was as if the door had vanished and been replaced by a seamless, solid, shelf-lined wall. The outline of the door was perfectly hidden in the natural seams between the logs, and the hinges and opening mechanism must have been disguised by the built-in shelves.

"Amazing. You'd never guess it was anything but a wall," I remarked. "It opens from the outside as well?"

"Just from the inside, I think," Chef K replied. "If I plan to come in from the outside, I leave it disengaged just a hair so I can push it open."

Brady had unhooked the skis from my chair so I could wheel myself around again, and I did a full turn, taking in the room. If you didn't know about the hidden exterior entrance, you'd just think it was a regular large pantry. The only thing unusual about it was the odd mix of old and new construction. The wall with the hidden door and the exposed-beam ceiling were clearly as old as the original lodge, but the food-filled floor-to-ceiling shelving units on the other two walls, and the interior door across from us, looked brand-new. The shelves were covered with all kinds of interesting foodstuffs, including a lot of raw vegetables, like beets, winter squash, and cabbage (thankfully still fresh and un-stinky!). Strands of dried peppers, garlic, and herbs hung from the ceiling.

Everything was well organized, but any fantasies I'd had about a secret door leading to a chamber full of the lodge's legendary hidden gold quickly vanished. It was clearly a food pantry. At least that's what it was now that Chef K had discovered it.

"Is this the hidden room they uncovered during the renovation?" I asked, taking a guess that this was the chamber Henry had told me about.

Chef K nodded. "The workers found it when

they tore down the old wall to put in the storage and freezer space under the restaurant, so I had them put it to good use."

"Henry told me Mrs. Bosley thought finding a secret room proved her theory that there was hidden treasure somewhere in the lodge from the old gold rush days," I said. I was still hoping the room might hold clues to the golden nugget that had somehow wound up in Clark's pocket. Maybe Chef K knew something that Henry didn't.

"Oh, yeah, sure, we found a treasure chest full of gold," Chef K deadpanned so convincingly I nearly got my hopes up. "But a leprechaun riding a unicorn ran off with it." She rolled her eyes. "What they found was dust, dirt, and a perfectly cool, dry space with a natural earthen floor for me to use in place of a root cellar."

"A root cellar with a hidden door no one but you is supposed to know about," Liz observed. "How convenient."

"I didn't know the door was there until the

renovation was done," she explained. "I had the contractor leave the back wall exposed because it already had shelves built in. I found the door by accident a few weeks later when I was trying to fix a loose shelf."

"But why not tell anyone?" I asked.

"Why would I?" she countered, as if I'd just asked her the silliest question ever. "This way I can go in and out of the lodge without having to be annoyed by anybody or answer any stupid questions."

"And here I thought you were a people person," Liz muttered.

Chef K's clandestine use of a clandestine door did seem less suspicious given how antisocial she was. Now I was more interested in the room itself. A secret door leading into a previously hidden chamber could be hiding other secrets as well.

"So you never had a chance to explore the other two walls to see if there was anything hidden behind the new shelving too?" I asked.

"I don't have time for fairy tales, and I'm definitely not letting anyone mess with my brand-new custom shelves," she warned. "What does this have to do with whoever is trying to ruin my restaurant?"

"I don't know," I admitted. "Someone paid Clark a gold nugget to sabotage you, and there's a chance it could be related to Mrs. Bosley's old legend."

"So basically you have no idea who's out to get me or why?" she grumbled.

"No, but with your help I'm going to find out," I told her. She may not have been the easiest person to work with, but it's always a good idea to remain polite—even when the victim is not. "Let's start with who else might know about the secret door to set that trap."

"Unless somebody saw me from outside, I don't have any idea," she said. "I never use it during work hours, when my staff is around. Plenty of them have access to the pantry, so I guess it's possible someone else discovered it on their own, but my people would never do something like this."

"You're a great cook, but you're not exactly the nicest boss," Liz pointed out.

Chef K started to snarl but relaxed into a sigh.

"Okay, maybe I could treat them a little better sometimes, but do you really think someone would want to *hurt me* just because I yell too much? They'd be sabotaging their own jobs, and a lot of them chose to come with me from New York. My people get paid well, they get a better education with me than in any culinary school, and they get to put working for me on their résumé."

"So the next chef they work for knows they need a hug?" Liz prodded.

"So the next chef they work for knows they're pros who can handle the stress of working in a topflight kitchen for a topflight chef," she countered. "Everyone who makes it to my kitchen either stays or they graduate to higher positions at other top restaurants. More than a few go on to run kitchens of their own."

From what I'd seen and heard, it was mostly true. Her employees might not like her, but they did seem to respect her and take real pride in the quality of Mountain to Table's food. And that food really was topflight (if you actually got a chance to eat it in between all the mayhem!).

Clark might have been letting someone pay him to pull his strings, but he didn't seem to have anything against her personally, even with all the yelling, and I think he saw the hot towels and the greenhouse as fairly harmless pranks. I couldn't see him doing something as extreme as setting that trap. So who would?

"What about other employees at the lodge?" I asked. "Anyone who might have a grudge against you for some reason?"

"I don't really mingle," she said. "Besides, no one is allowed on restaurant turf except my people. I made sure of that the second I arrived. And that includes Leach and Alexander."

"So you're saying a restaurant outsider wouldn't have had access to the hidden door from the kitchen. That would mean it's either an inside job, or someone's been watching you for a while," I concluded. I looked down at my watch. I was out of time. I had a "hack-off" conference call to get to. "Keep your eyes open and let me know if you see anything suspicious. I have some other leads I'm working as well, and I'll let you know what I turn up."

"Hey, can we use the secret door in here to get back to the lodge?" Brady asked. "It was not easy getting here the other way."

Chef K nodded and moved aside so we could go through the pantry's new not-secret door.

"Um, hey, uh, Nancy," Chef K said as I started to wheel myself away. "Um, thank you."

I could tell it wasn't easy for her to say. I had been starting to think Chef K's interior was as gruff as her exterior, but all it took was a simple thank-you to remind me that she was a human being with feelings too.

I turned back to her and smiled. "We're going to find out what's going on and get Mountain to Table running smoothly, I promise."

"I have a lot riding on this place," she confessed. "Going to a middle-of-nowhere wilderness to open a restaurant is a big risk. I believe in Archie's vision, and I want to do something as a chef that no one else has ever done. But that trap . . . I feel like I'm being hunted, and . . . I'm scared. Part of me wants to pack up my knives and head back to the city, but my entire reputation hinges on this."

That was when Liz wrapped her arms around Chef K and gave her a big hug. Chef K froze with her arms at her side like she'd never been hugged before and didn't know what to do, but then she tentatively lifted up her arms and squeezed back.

"We got your back, girl," Liz said.

"Um, do you guys want to take some snacks back with you?" Chef K asked shyly once Liz let her go.

The door lead us right to Mountain to Table's pantry. We left with an amazing picnic basket full of gourmet snacks, including a mason jar of perfectly crunchy *not*-rotten sauerkraut that was actually so delicious I ended up eating it straight out of the jar with a fork!

I was back in my suite, munching on sesame-seed-stuffed Greek dolmas wrapped in handpicked wild grape leaves, when the alarm on my phone buzzed. It was hack-off time!

I flipped open my tablet, tapped the Google

Hangouts app icon, and joined the video call George had set up. Everyone's pictures popped up with a *ding*, including Bess, who wasn't part of the challenge but insisted on being there for "moral support," she said, although I suspected she just didn't want to be left out.

"All right, guys!" I said, kicking off the introductions. "George and Bess of Team Drew, meet Frank and Joe of Team Hardy."

Bess said a breezy hello to everyone and batted her eyes. Joe practically melted off the screen. Bess kind of has that effect on guys. Frank started to melt too, which wouldn't have been so surprising—only I think it was George's own "hey" he was melting at!

George seemed oblivious to it, in normal George fashion, and launched right into her results.

"Okay, we know the old owners' son, Dino Bosley, and Sheriff Pruitt both stand to make a lot of money if the lodge caves on the pipeline and they can lease their land. They also have a long history together, going back to sharing All-Conference honors for the Prospect High Prospectors football team. As an adult,

Dino Bosley has a long troublemaking rap sheet in Prospect—or at least he would have a rap sheet if his friend the sheriff didn't keep letting him off the hook. According to the local police blotter, he's been arrested at least ten times for everything from reckless driving to assault to disorderly conduct, and not one of them resulted in charges."

"Well, we know for a fact that Pruitt plays fast and loose with how he enforces the law," Frank said bitterly. "So you think they're working on something shady together involving the pipeline?"

"Could be, or could be Pruitt is covering for his old friend Dino," George speculated. "Who it turns out may have another bone to pick with the lodge as well. Dino had been in talks with a restaurant owner in town about partnering up to revamp the lodge's prime restaurant space, which we now know as Mountain to Table. The venture got far enough that it was announced in the local paper just a few weeks before Leach and Alexander swooped in and bought the lodge outright."

"Dashing Dino Bosley's dreams of being a big restaurateur," I theorized. "Which might give him a grudge against Chef K and Mountain to Table to go along with his pipeline beef."

"We'd been looking for a link tying the restaurant sabotage to the pipeline, and this could be a way of killing two birds with one hot pepper," George suggested.

"That's all you got?" Joe asked dismissively. "Frank, hit 'em with the big guns."

"We've got a new lead on your Representative Alexander, and it's a doozy," Frank announced. "We know there's a lot of political pressure on him to cave to the pipeline. Well, from the looks of it, the possibly-not-so-esteemed gentleman from Montana may have more than just a political interest in the lodge leasing the land to the pipeline. He could have a financial one as well."

My stomach dropped as Frank paused to let this sink in before continuing.

"Harold Crane, a businessman with close ties

to Larry Thorwald, made a *huge* contribution to the Alexander reelection campaign right before he closed the deal on the lodge."

"Could it be a coincidence?" I asked. "That doesn't necessarily prove that Alexander knew about the connection. Politicians get donations from all kinds of people."

"Sure, but Crane is knee deep in the lobby to open protected wilderness to oil exploration, which makes him a pretty strange contributor to a pro-environment politician," Frank continued. "Especially one who owns a big stake in a new high-profile eco-resort that just happens to stand in the way of the pipeline's construction."

"So Alexander has been banking political capital with environmentally conscious voters while also banking money from a dude with a major anti-environment agenda," Joe commented.

"That's not all," said Frank. "The Leach and Alexander real estate firm bought a *big* chunk of stock in a manufacturing company called All Alloy right afterward. The company manufactures some parts used in solar panel construction, which on the surface doesn't seem too weird for a 'green' real estate development firm."

"But . . . ?" I asked tentatively, waiting for the other shoe to drop.

"Until you dig a little deeper," George cut in, "and learn that the same company is also one of the biggest suppliers of rivets to the pipeline company's main contractor." She leaned back with a smug grin. "Thought you were the only one with that lead, didn't ya?"

"Impressive," Frank admitted, blushing a little.

"Not that impressive," Joe grumbled.

"All Alloy's stock has been rising along with the pipeline company's," Frank continued. "And if this pipeline gets built, anyone who bought in before the project was green-lit could make a killing."

"And that now includes both Grant *and* your friend Archie, since their firm is sitting on the stock as well," George concluded.

"There's got to be a mix-up," I said, furrowing my

brow. "I know Archie wouldn't go for anything that benefited a pipeline company no matter how much profit was in it, and definitely not the pipeline company he's fighting against."

"You suspect he wouldn't, Nance, but you don't know for a fact," Bess pointed out.

Ugh, Bess was usually the trusting one.

"Hey, my cynicism is finally rubbing off on you!" George declared cheerily.

I sighed. Bess wasn't being cynical, though; she was simply being objective. I really respected Archie, but I couldn't let my personal feelings bias my investigation.

"I'm going to have to have a heart-to-heart with Archie to see what he knows," I conceded.

"What we know is that there are conflicts of interest up the wazoo with the Grand Sky Lodge and the pipeline, but what is the connection between that and all the sabotage and break-ins?" Joe asked.

"And the gold nugget!" Bess chimed in, and I had to smile. Bess was a sucker for jewelry, even if it was still in the raw-material stage.

I brought them up to date on the discovery of the hidden entrance to the lodge and my interview with Chef K, not that it answered any of our questions. We had a ton of clues, but most of them just raised more questions. And there were more than enough suspects, but it was hard to match their motives with the crimes.

"Sabotaging the lodge might make sense for a pipeline supporter, but why target the restaurant specifically?" I asked.

"Unless you're Dino," George reminded us. "He's pro pipeline, he has a reason to have a grudge against the restaurant, and he did show up to make a scene right before the hot-towel incident that started all of it."

"And if he used to work there, he could still have an accomplice on the inside," added Bess.

"But what would that have to do with Grant Alexander?" Joe asked.

"And there's also the fact that it was Grant's suite that was broken into most recently," I interjected—another complication. "He's been targeted as well, so he's a break-in victim, not a perpetrator. Archie, too. The sabotage could ruin the lodge's whole grand opening."

"At least that's the way they want to make it look," Joe speculated.

"It doesn't make sense," I said. "They both have too much invested in this week."

"I took the fall for somebody, and I want to know who," Frank cut in. "I don't know if it was Grant Alexander, but he was hiding something, and it sure looked like Sheriff Pruitt was covering up for him."

"The whole thing seems fishy from Dino on down," Bess said.

"Smoked fishy," Joe agreed, earning odd looks from Bess and George.

"Sounds like we still have a lot more questions than answers," I said, my head spinning with all the variables.

"One fact I think we can all agree on is that Frank won the hack-off," Joe declared.

"You're dreaming, Hardy. I totally crushed him!" George objected immediately.

"Only if by 'crushed' you mean 'didn't do as well as,'" Joe shot back.

"You're just upset because your brother got whupped by a girl," George snapped.

"Dude, my bro stomped all over you in a totally equal-opportunity, gender-nonspecific way," Joe argued.

"Dude yourself, dude, the only one who did any stompage was me," George retorted.

"Okay, okay, you both win!" I cut in before we spent the rest of my stay arguing over who had out-hacked who.

"But Frank wins more," said Joe smugly.

"Actually, I think George did some really great research," Frank gushed.

"Victory is mine!" George proclaimed.

"Traitor," Joe mumbled.

Bess and I met eyes and smiled. George might have been oblivious to it, but it sure looked to us like she had an admirer.

"So what's next on your end of the investigation?" I asked Joe and Frank, trying to return the conversation to the topic at hand.

"I'll keep tailing Thorwald to see who else he meets

with," Joe said. "He's been in town greasing palms all over the place."

"Joe will be keeping his distance, though," Frank said pointedly. "The guy hangs out with a couple of nasty-looking bodyguards."

"I think I saw them on the way into town," I shared, cringing at the thought of the two beefy thugs who'd escorted the expensively dressed businessman from the town hall. "Is Thorwald the one with the fancy overcoat?"

"That's him," Frank confirmed.

"Then distance is definitely called for," I agreed. "Those guys were no joke."

"Yeah, they're both nicknamed Tiny, apparently," said Joe.

"Doesn't that get confusing?" Bess asked.

"One's Tiny Tony and the other's Tiny Ronnie," Joe explained.

Bess giggled.

"They're a lot more terrifying than they sound," Frank warned. "And they've been known to pound the heads of any protesters who get too close to their boss."

"Be careful," I cautioned. "We've already had a Hardy boy locked up on this case; we don't want the other to end up in the hospital."

CHAPTER FIFTEEN

❧

On the Edge

I TRUSTED THE BOYS TO LOOK OUT FOR themselves. The mission that had me really nervous was mine. Could my seemingly earnest eco-resort host Archie secretly be hedging his bets and setting himself up to profit off the pipeline? I was about to find out.

I rolled into the reading room down the hall from Grant's suite, where Henry told me I could find Archie.

It was a beautiful old room with built-in book-shelves reaching all the way up to the high ceilings and a little reading nook in the corner. It even had one of those rolling staircases you could push around to reach books on the highest shelves.

Archie was in front of the fire in a big leather chair with reading glasses on, reviewing some paperwork. He looked up and smiled as I wheeled myself in.

"Nancy!" he exclaimed. "How's your leg?"

"It feels okay. My ankle hurts, but it's not too bad, and my upper leg doesn't really hurt at all," I said, neglecting to mention my heart hurting at the thought of the interrogation I was about to give him.

I shivered a little, a draft of cool air giving my broken leg a chill through the sock covering the exposed toes at the end of my cast as I rolled past the bookshelves to get closer to the fire.

"Good! At least I don't have to feel guilty about causing you too much pain," he said. "Any news on the case?"

I took a deep breath. "What do you know about the company All Alloy?"

"All Alloy?" He took a moment to think, or at least that was how he wanted it to look. "They're a solar panel parts manufacturer, I believe. I think we have some of their stock in the firm's investment portfolio. Are you . . ." Archie took off his glasses. "Nancy, why would you be looking into our investments?"

"Because this one is also the main supplier of a key part used in the construction of the pipeline," I informed him.

"They're what?!" Archie blurted. "If that's true, I'm glad you caught it. I'll have Grant tell our broker to divest it right away. Our portfolio is supposed to be strictly clean and green, but it can be hard to vet every company entirely."

Archie's surprise appeared to be genuine, but appearances can be deceiving.

"Why have Grant call the broker? Why not do it yourself?" I inquired.

"Grant briefs me on where our money is going, but he's more hands-on with the firm's investments and the financial side of things, while I focus on daily operations and development," Archie explained. "Much of the vision for what we do is mine, but Grant's always been the better business mind."

"Is it the kind of business mind that would hedge its bets so the firm still makes a profit if the pipeline goes through?" I asked.

Archie tensed up in his seat like it had been him I'd accused. "Absolutely not! That would go against everything this lodge and our firm stand for. I'm sure this is just an unfortunate oversight."

"So you and Grant always see eye to eye on things?" I asked, thinking about the argument I'd witnessed between them through the window of Grant's suite right after I broke my leg.

"Well, er, I don't think any business partners agree all the time, of course," he said. "But largely, yes, we share the same overall vision."

"I saw the two of you arguing after the opening ceremony," I told him. "And it looked pretty heated."

"Were you spying on us, Nancy?" he asked, looking genuinely hurt.

"I'm sorry, I didn't mean to, but I saw you through the window and I'd heard that there'd been death threats against both of you because of the pipeline and

I was concerned," I told him. "And now that there's an active investigation, it sounds like whatever you were arguing about may be relevant to the case."

Archie sighed. "Grant was upset about my plan to turn our backcountry land into a permanent nature conservancy. And to be fair, I'd just had the idea that morning and should have discussed it with him before making the announcement, but . . ."

"But . . . ?" I prompted him when he fell silent.

"Grant has been urging me to keep our options open with the lease to the pipeline," he confessed, not meeting my eyes. "Which I obviously rejected, by the way. I'm sure the only reason he'd even consider it is because of all the political pressure he's under. He represents a lot of different constituents, and many of them are for it, including a lot of people in town. I don't agree and think it's shortsighted, but I admit that there are some persuasive arguments, and I understand why some people are for it."

"But that goes against your whole mission!" I objected.

"Which is exactly why I've stood my ground and insisted we have to keep the interests of the lodge and Grant's political career separate," he said. "I do think it's important, though, to try to understand where people are coming from. That way you can have compassion for them and better explain your point of view so they can see how it actually benefits them, too."

"I don't think you're going to have much luck changing the minds of Dino Bosley or Sheriff Pruitt, no matter what you say," I shared.

He nodded sadly. "Some people are so set in the way they think, you may never get through to them, even if the thing they think they want just hurts them and the town in the end. But I believe there are people who really will listen if you treat them fairly and give them a chance."

"And what about Grant? Did he listen?" I asked.

"Grant doesn't want the pipeline either, he's just in a difficult position," he said. "And to be honest, the lodge is as well."

"But you have all the leverage!" I reminded him.

"You own the land the pipeline needs, and there's nothing they can do to make you give it to them if you don't want to."

"Yes, it looks that way, thankfully. The pipeline company wants to get this deal done fast or shift gears and find another location. Our position appears strong on paper, and there's no reason for them to think we can't just wait them out. And if we succeed in stopping them here, it may inspire others to stand up to them in the next location too. . . ." Archie let the sentence trail off.

"Exactly!" I agreed. "Shutting them down here would be a huge victory for the whole conservation movement."

Archie pinched the bridge of his nose. "Only we had to borrow a lot more money than we expected to renovate the lodge the way I dreamed it. If the Grand Sky Lodge doesn't open strong and generate enough income to cover costs right away, we may not be able to repay the loans."

My eyes went wide. I'd known remaking the lodge

as an eco-resort had been expensive, but not so expensive that they were in financial trouble before they even opened! No wonder Archie was so anxious over the sabotage. He had a lot more at stake than just bad publicity and a rocky start.

"The firm is so heavily leveraged that we could lose the entire business along with the lodge," he continued. "If it gets off to a slow start and we can't raise more emergency capital, we could be forced to either lease that one small sliver of land to the pipeline—or risk losing all of it."

My stomach sank. "If they knew how precarious your financial situation really is, they could just wait *you* out."

"And I'm afraid we could be left with few options if they did," Archie revealed, hanging his head. "They're offering a huge sum of money. And Grant is right that in a worst-case scenario, we could use that money to do a lot of good. Not just to save the lodge and see our vision succeed; we'd have a windfall left over to reinvest in all kinds of new conservation efforts." Archie paused, shaking his head like he was trying to erase the thought from his mind. "But it would mean compromising my core values and contributing to the destruction of the very same natural resources I pledged to protect."

I could see the internal debate tormenting him as he stood up and started pacing in front of the fire.

"I wanted to create the land conservancy to take the decision out of our hands and make that option impossible," Archie declared. "That way the land would be protected even if we aren't, and we'd be forced to find another way. It wouldn't be the first time we had to fight from behind to make a project work."

"That's really admirable, standing up for your principles and putting the future of the land over your own success," I said. "A lot of people would never even think to do that."

"But I didn't really think it all the way through before rushing to announce it," he said sadly. "As Grant pointed out, turning hundreds of acres of lodge-owned land into a forever-wild nature preserve that can't be developed is basically the same as giving it away as far as investors are concerned. The property value of the entire resort could take a huge hit, making it impossible to raise the money we may need to save it. I hate to admit it, but he's right."

It was a complicated predicament, that was for sure. Archie's attempt to do the right thing and save the land from exploitation could indirectly lead to the failure of his vision for an environmentally sustainable eco-resort.

"I also didn't take into account how much the move would hurt Grant politically," Archie added. "Refusing to lease the land to the pipeline is one thing—Grant could always defend it by deflecting the blame to me and saying his hands were tied—but him agreeing to turn it into a nature preserve? A lot of his supporters, including many of the important ones he relies on to get reelected, would see that as an aggressive act to block the pipeline against their interests."

"You mean like Harry Crane?" I asked.

"I don't know who that is," replied Archie.

"A backroom oil lobbyist who's been helping fund the push to exploit protected wilderness areas all over the country," I informed him reluctantly—if he honestly didn't know, I didn't want to add to his torment. "He's basically a professional anticonservationist."

"That can't be right," Archie stated.

"He's also a close associate of Larry Thorwald," I said, dropping the second part of the equation on him.

"I can't believe Grant knew about this," Archie insisted. "Yes, he was considering leasing the land, but only as a last resort. He would never take money from those people. It goes against everything our firm and this lodge set out to achieve. It has to be a coincidence."

I'd thought so at first too when Frank told me. Political campaigns take contributions from all kinds of people. But—

"It sure is a funny one, especially when you combine it with the All Alloy stock purchase," I reminded him. "You'd almost think he had insider info on the pipeline's plans."

"I refuse to believe it," Archie said. "Grant and

I have been friends and partners for decades. I can't imagine he would help them sabotage my dream for financial gain."

Sabotage. There was that word again. What I still didn't know was what Grant's apparent involvement with the pipeline had to do with the attacks on the restaurant and Chef K. Not to mention the break-ins. Could it be another tactic to put pressure on the lodge to lease the land?

"Grant went back to the state capital for a meeting," Archie said before I could pose the theory to him. "The two of us are going to have a long conversation and get to the bottom of all this as soon as he gets back tomorrow."

"I'd like to interview him as well," I said.

"No," Archie said firmly. "This is personal, and I'm going to handle it myself."

He walked out of the room before I could argue. I was going to have to trust Archie with this part of the investigation for now—at least I hoped I could trust him.

He'd just admitted that he might be forced to decide between leasing the land to the pipeline and saving the lodge, and if he did, his firm could make a pretty penny off the All Alloy stock he said he didn't know made parts for the pipeline.

With as much action as the five days had seen, I was prepared for something crazy to happen at any minute, but the rest of the day turned out to be shockingly uneventful. No new discoveries, gold nuggets, hidden doors, or, thankfully, sabotage! And as much action as *I'd* seen the last few days, I was exhausted. And since getting to bed early was literally what the doctor ordered, I figured it was about time I followed Doc Sherman's advice.

Besides, I wanted to be up bright and early the next morning to watch the sun rise—and to watch Brady shoot footage of Liz teaching the kids how to ski for their documentary! They planned to hit the slopes before they officially opened for the day to take advantage of the beautiful morning light while they still had the mountain all to themselves.

I wheeled myself over to the bathroom to brush my teeth. Before I left the lodge hospital, a nurse had patiently showed me how to get things done from the wheelchair. At her suggestion, I had a paper cup ready at the sink so I could rinse without standing up.

Then I reversed the chair back into bedroom and positioned it next to my bed. I'd also learned how to move from my wheelchair to a bed or a chair. My transfers still weren't perfect, but I was able to use my right leg and arms to swing my body from one seated position to another. From there it was just a matter of lifting my cast onto the bed.

I smiled once I was all tucked in. It certainly wasn't easy to learn all this stuff, but I was proud of myself for getting here.

I woke up well rested and excited to take a short break from the investigation. I transferred to my wheelchair and made my way over to the window looking out on the slopes, armed with my iPad, my walkie-talkie, and my now-trusty binoculars. I'd gotten to spend enough time looking through them the past few days that I practically had the mountain memorized!

Seeing the first light break over the mountain was downright glorious. Brady was still getting set up, and I couldn't see Liz and the kids through the binoculars—the slope they were shooting on was just out of view—but I could see Liz checking each Thing's gear through one of the camera angles on my iPad.

Brady had me hooked up with a live stream of all the different camera angles. He was going to be skiing along with them, shooting as he went, but he also had remote cameras set up at different places on the trails along with the drone. Liz and the kids were even wearing small GoPro action cameras to film their points of view too. I had my walkie-talkie tuned in to the radio channel they were using for the tiny remote radios they wore in their helmets, so I could listen in as Brady gave them direction.

I looked through the binoculars again to catch the rest of the sunrise over the empty mountain, and I noticed it wasn't entirely empty anymore. A well-bundled skier was getting ready to drop in on a nearby slope on the western edge of the mountain that everyone called Round Top because of the little dome at the top of the trail. The mountain hadn't opened yet, so the skier must have been an employee or someone else with permission to ski, though there was no way to tell who it was, with the full-face ski mask they were wearing. Whoever they were, they were lucky! What a beautiful time to ski. The sunrise had turned the freshly groomed snow a gorgeous golden hue. The scene would have made a beautiful painting.

Except, I realized as I traced with my binoculars the run the skier was about to take, something was off. I'd spent enough time staring at the mountains through the binoculars to notice something about the trail was different, but it took me a minute to figure out what.

Some of the ski boundary signs had been moved. They were now in the middle of the old trail, changing the course of the run about halfway down. I didn't think much of it at first—I figured the groomers had just decided to make some changes—until I followed the new course with my binoculars.

Right off the side of the mountain! And the skier was already on their way down with no way to warn them!

CHAPTER SIXTEEN

✦

Wipeout!

IF THE SKIER FOLLOWED THE BOUNDARY signs, he or she was going to plummet off a twenty-foot ledge!

I stared helplessly at the doomed skier. The slopes still weren't open, so there was no ski patrol in sight, and the only other people on the mountain were Brady, Liz, and the kids. I could see Brady a couple of slopes over, heading back toward the kids, who were goofing around at the top of the same slope where I'd seen them earlier, but I couldn't see Liz on any of the camera angles.

The only thing I could think to do was to radio them.

"Brady! Liz! Come in! There's a skier in trouble on Round Top! They're about to go off the side!" I yelled into the walkie-talkie, but all I got in response was static. Had they even heard my call for help?

I frantically tried switching the channels, trying to find ski patrol dispatch, yelling, "Mayday! Mayday! Rescue emergency on Round Top!" over and over again into each channel in case anyone heard.

"Nancy, is that you?" Henry's voice buzzed over the walkie-talkie.

"Henry!" I shouted. "Get ski patrol to Round Top now! Someone moved the trail markers, and there's a skier headed straight for the ledge!"

"Oh my, but how—" Henry started to ask, but I cut him off.

"There's no time! Get help now!"

"On it!" he said, clicking off.

Even if Henry reached ski patrol right away, there would never be enough time for them to get up the slope before the skier reached the ledge. All they'd be able to do was hope the person was still alive to rescue at the bottom.

I picked the binoculars back up with shaking hands. Stuck in my suite in a wheelchair, there was nothing more I could do but watch. The skier was closing in on the halfway point, mere yards from the moved boundary signs, seconds away from launching themselves over the side.

I couldn't watch. I was about to shut my eyes to block out the inevitable fall when there was a flash of movement farther up the slope at the edge of my binoculars' field of vision.

Liz! Her ponytail waved in the air behind her as she swooped down from a steeper merging trail and rocketed toward the condemned skier. And what a turn! She carved hard, going nearly parallel to the snow, then dropped herself into a controlled skid-out right in front of the unsuspecting skier, wiping them both out mere feet from the ledge!

The skier hit the ground *hard*—but thanks to

Liz, it was ground they hit and not air! As bad as the wipeout looked, the skier was still in one piece. They wouldn't have any idea how close they'd come to going over the edge. And the only reason they hadn't was because of Liz's daring rescue—so daring that she'd risked going over herself if she'd misjudged her skid even a little.

I watched through the binoculars as Liz sat up, dusted herself off, and lifted herself back onto her skis. The other skier leaped up with their back to me, whipped off their mask, and started yelling at Liz. Liz pointed and the skier turned, revealing their shocked face as they gaped at the ledge a few feet away.

Chef K. As soon as I saw her face, I knew the moved signs weren't an accident. Someone had tried to take her out.

She stood there, silently staring over the ledge at the fate Liz had saved her from. This time it was Chef K who embraced Liz with a hug.

Watching the scene unfold through my binoculars, I realized something else. Chef K had also been the person originally scheduled to go down the trail where I broke my leg during the opening day's inaugural run. Markers had been put in the wrong place that day too, and if Chef K hadn't canceled at the last minute, she would have been the one to wipe out on the ice because of it, not me.

My "accident" hadn't been an accident at all. Someone had set a trap to take out the chef, and I'd just had the bad luck of stepping in it.

The unmarked patch of ice that broke my leg hadn't been a mere groomer's mistake, and I was pretty sure that whoever set that trap had set this one as well. But who? Chef K had been scheduled for the inaugural ceremony before I took her place, so a ton of people would have known about it—but this was just a random morning with a whole mountain full of different trails. To get the answer, I'd need to find out who knew that Chef K was going to be the first one down Round Top that morning.

"Nancy!" Henry's voice buzzed over the walkie-talkie. "Ski patrol is on their way!"

"They're okay, Henry! Liz saved Chef K from going over the edge!" I called back.

"Chef K?!" he gasped. "It wasn't an accident, was it?"

"Not likely," I replied. "Once ski patrol checks them out, have them tell Chef and Liz to meet me in the ski lounge."

Henry buzzed back not long after to tell me they were on the way. Luckily, neither of them had suffered anything more than bumps and bruises.

The lodge didn't fare as well. The entire mountain was temporarily shut down while the groomers and ski patrol raced around, making sure none of the other slopes had been tampered with. Sure enough, it was only the one Chef K had skied down.

When I ran into Archie in the hall, he was beside himself. Not only had his star chef almost been taken out of commission, but also, closing the slopes for even a few hours was a major blow to business—especially with the lodge scheduled to close for the holidays the next day. The staff had been instructed to keep the details of the "accident" private, but it turned out some of the guests had actually watched the rescue live over one of the trail cams the lodge streams on their website. Word got out, and a lot of the remaining guests—the ones who hadn't already checked out after the hot towel, flaming menorah, and sauerkraut stink bomb incidents—were calling their vacation quits.

Of course Carol Fremont was already tweeting and 'gramming about it. George, Bess, and I had decided these crimes had become way bigger than just a reporter trying to land a cover story. We agreed she could be safely crossed off the suspect list, but that didn't mean she couldn't do any damage.

And Carol's tweet-storm wasn't the only storm hitting the lodge.

That big winter storm my dad had warned me about? The latest weather reports had come in, and they weren't good. The storm had picked up steam and was poised to hit that night, a full twenty-four hours earlier than predicted! That meant even more guests were scrambling to book earlier flights and reschedule travel plans to make sure they were able to get home in time for Christmas.

The following day was Christmas Eve, after all. Everyone was supposed to check out by noon so the lodge's employees could take the holiday off, but it didn't look like that many guests would even be left. The slow start Archie had dreaded was all but guaranteed. And there could be a lot of bad publicity going into the new year on top of it. It was a perfect storm of bad news for the Grand Sky Lodge. There was no way around it. The opening week had been a bona fide disaster.

Or it would be if I couldn't solve the case and set things right before my flight the following afternoon. With any luck, this winter wonderland could be disaster-free before Christmas.

Archie was already reeling, and when I told him my opening day "accident" hadn't been an accident either, he literally stumbled backward and had to sit down. I assured him we were going to find out who was behind this and turn the lodge's bad start around. Then I headed for the ski lounge, hoping I was right.

· · ·

I got big hugs from both Liz *and* Chef K as soon as I rolled in.

"If you hadn't spotted me, I would have . . ." Chef K trailed off, hugging me again instead.

"Liz deserves most of the credit. She's the one who swooped in like a superhero!" I said. "That was one of the most amazing rescues I've ever seen, and believe me, I've seen more than a few."

Liz actually blushed. "It was nothing. Sorry I didn't radio back. I was afraid I wouldn't have time, and Brady's radio cut out. They're still having trouble with signals getting crossed on the hill."

"I'm just glad you heard the call!" I assured her.

"Brady's totally stoked because I was wearing my helmet cam, so we have it on video for the documentary," Liz shared, grinning. "He wanted us to go down again and reenact it so he could get a wide shot too, but Chef growled at him."

Chef just smiled and rolled her eyes.

I felt bad that it took being scared to death to bring

it out of her, but I was liking this new, kinder, more fun Chef K.

"I'm just glad you're both okay. The trick now is to make sure you stay that way," I told them, turning to Chef K. "Who knew you'd be the first one to ski down Round Top this morning?"

"I take a sunrise run down one of the intermediate slopes every morning before the mountain opens, to clear my mind when no one else is around to annoy me," she said in typical Chef K style.

"Don't you have to get permission from ski patrol first?" Liz asked. "We had to get clearance on each of the slopes we planned to shoot on, and ski patrol only approved it because Brady and I are both expert skiers with emergency rescue training."

"I made Archie tell ski patrol to give me permission," she asserted. "Marni or one of the others usually checks with the groomers and messages me the night before to tell me which slope is cleared for me each day, and they have me wear a radio and a beacon in case anything goes wrong."

"So anyone on ski patrol or the grooming crew might potentially know," I summarized. "That narrows the pool down a bit, but not by much. Was it Marni who messaged you last night?"

"Yeah, it was," Chef K confirmed.

"Okay, good," I said, happy to have a reason to catch up with Marni. I had been so busy with the case that I hadn't seen her since she saved me from that snowbank on the first day. "When she gets off her shift, I can ask her which of the ski patrollers and groomers knew what slope you'd be on and who else they might have told."

I wished it were under different circumstances, but it would still be nice to see her friendly face.

"In the meantime," I said, pointing my chair toward the door, "I'm going to track down Henry and see what I can find out about that trail cam."

I found him in his usual spot at the front desk.

"I don't see how a live stream of the mountain will help us figure out who moved the trail markers a few hours after the fact," Henry commented, walking around the desk to lead me to the office of the Grand Sky Lodge's tech gal, Dominique.

"The live stream won't," I replied. "But if we're lucky, there will be an archive."

Dominique's office had the same exposed logs as the rest of the lodge, only this room was filled to the gills with modern computer equipment, including a monitor showing four different live trail cams looking at the mountain from different angles.

"You're in luck," Dominique told us. "The system automatically archives everything for twenty-four hours before deleting itself to make room for the next day's footage."

She punched a button, zooming in on a camera angle that captured three different slopes on the left side of the mountain, with Round Top visible on the far left. The slopes were still closed for inspection, so the only people you could see in the live feed were groomers and ski patrol.

"Can you zoom in tighter on Round Top and take us back before sunrise?" I asked.

Dominique clicked one key on her keyboard to focus on the image and another to rewind. The image wasn't as crystal clear zoomed in, and you couldn't see any facial details, but it was still close enough to pick out the ski patrol outfits from the groomers in civilian clothes.

The footage sped up as Dominique rewound, Liz's rescue of Chef K zipping by backward as the sun moved in reverse.

The footage got a whole lot darker and grainier as soon as the sun was gone. You could still see the contrast of the slope on the mountain, but making out details was a lot harder. Even if we spotted someone, it could be difficult to identify them. Maybe there'd still be other clues, though. The time stamp on the video had just zipped past an hour before dawn when a little blip shot across the screen.

"Pause there!" I cried.

The speed returned to normal just as a figure emerged from the back side of Round Top.

"It's the saboteur!" Henry gasped. "But they're all in shadow!"

"Can you zoom in further?" I asked.

"It's going to be pretty pixelated," Dominique warned.

She was right. It would have been hard to make out any detail at all—if it weren't for the contrast of the large white ski patrol cross on the person's jacket and the long braided ponytail flowing from the back of her helmet.

My heart sank. There was only one ski patroller with a long braid like that: Marni.

CHAPTER SEVENTEEN

Oh What Fun It Is

"IT WASN'T ME, I SWEAR!" MARNI PLEADED, her signature long braid swaying as a deputy led her toward the police cruiser in handcuffs. The same thing had happened to Frank a few days earlier, only this time the Prospect PD really did have probable cause to make an arrest.

"Save it for the judge," the deputy spat. "We've got you on camera, and 'I was sleeping the whole time' is just about the weakest alibi I've ever heard."

"But this doesn't make any sense," Marni wailed. "My whole life is about helping people! Why would I want to hurt Chef K? I'm one of the only people who actually likes her!"

"She's right, it doesn't make sense," I told Archie, my heart sinking all over again as we watched from inside the doorway. "I wish you would have let me interrogate her before the police got here. I can't think of what her motive would be. It just doesn't feel right."

I'd been on enough cases to know that the nicest people can turn out to be some of the most devious criminals. Still, I couldn't reconcile the sweet person who'd boosted my confidence before my first ski run and rescued me afterward as the same person who'd knowingly sent me into the trap in the first place.

I'd tried to get Archie to let me question her myself, but he'd insisted on having the police waiting at the bottom of the mountain to put her in cuffs the second she came off the slopes.

"This isn't hot peppers and stink bombs anymore—this is a dangerous person, and I want the cops handling it," Archie said, repeating the same thing he'd told me after I'd shown him the trail-cam video of our braided suspect moving the ski boundary signs that had nearly sent Chef K over a twenty-foot ledge. "There will be plenty of time for the police and prosecutors to question her once she's safely behind bars."

"I've faced criminals who have done a lot worse," I reminded him. "Whatever happened before, Marni and I have a rapport, and she's more likely to open up to me than the people prosecuting her."

"I know you're fond of Marni; everyone was, including me," he assured me. "I don't know why she would do this, but Chef K could have been severely hurt, or worse. And her actions have caused you enough harm already. I'm not about to take any more chances."

"I don't know why either, and that's what's bugging me," I urged him. "All I need is a few minutes to talk to her. I'll have a better chance of getting a confession than Sheriff Pruitt will, that's for sure. And if she really did it, we can find out why and wrap the sabotage case up for good."

"The case *is* wrapped up," he asserted. "I wish it weren't true, but we both saw it on video with our own eyes this time. This vendetta against Chef K has cost us a fortune. I care less about why she did it than the fact that she's locked up where she can't do any more harm."

Marni looked pleadingly at us through the back-seat window of the cop car as it pulled away.

Archie sighed, glanced at his watch, and turned back to the lobby. "I have a lot of damage control to do, and more than enough to talk about with Grant when his car gets here from the airport."

I stared at the police car as it grew smaller in the distance, escorting Marni to the Prospect jail a few miles below. We had her on video. You couldn't see her face, so it wasn't 100 percent conclusive, but it was pretty damning—possibly damning enough to get a conviction and send her to prison for a long time. I just couldn't figure out her motivation. Fear of getting caught might give her a motive for pretending every-thing was hunky-dory the day I arrived and letting me ski into the trap she'd meant for Chef K, but what was her motive for setting the trap in the first place? Why *would* Marni try to take out Chef K? Could someone have put her up to it? Was she a hired hitter like waiter Clark? Or was she the mysterious gold-nugget-dropping burglar who hired Clark? And what did she have to gain if she was? Did it have something to do with the pipeline and the lodge's financial problems? Or was the damage it did to the lodge just a by-product of the saboteur's vendetta against Chef K, like Archie seemed to think? One thing was certain—I wasn't going to get the answers from Marni.

There was someone else who was supposed to have known about what awaited me on the opening cere-mony run that broke my leg.

Archie had already made up his mind about what happened, so I turned to my number one CI, Henry, to set up a meet with Todd, whose negligent grooming had originally been blamed for my so-called accident. I couldn't go back to the scene of the crime to investi-gate it for myself, and any evidence would be groomed and skied into oblivion by now anyway. Having Todd walk me through how he'd groomed my slope for the inaugural run was my only way to re-create what the slope looked like before and after the ice warning flags were moved. *If* he told me the truth.

Thanks to Henry, it wasn't long before Todd and I were chatting over hot chocolate in Chef K's restaurant.

"I told everyone it wasn't my fault, and this proves it!" Todd pumped his fist when I told him why I wanted to meet, but then he took an embarrassed look at my cast and cut the celebration short. "I don't mean to sound happy about what happened to you or anything, and Marni being the one who did it really stinks. She was always really cool to me; it's crazy she would do that and then let me take the fall for it too."

"You're not entirely off the hook yet," I cautioned him. "Marni was arrested for trying to take out Chef K on Round Top this morning, but we still don't have any proof she tampered with the trail I wiped out on."

"Oh, I have proof," he boasted. I leaned forward to hear what he was going to say next. Could this be the smoking gun?

"I don't know if it was Marni, but someone

definitely for sure messed with that slope," he declared. "I knew I'd flagged the ice patch you hit, and I told my boss Big Steve someone must have moved the flags around. He wasn't hearing it, though, so I went back and dug a little deeper. We all knew that area tended to get a little icy sometimes, but when I cleared away the powder, there was a solid sheet of ice."

"That's not news," I informed him, my hopes for a smoking gun going up in smoke. "Marni told me it was a solid sheet of ice right after she rescued me. She said she almost wiped out on it too and blamed the grooming crew for putting the warning flags in the wrong place."

"Yeah, but this wasn't the kind of ice that occurs naturally on these slopes. It was almost like someone cleared away the powder after we were done, poured water over it, then covered it back up to hide it," Todd explained. "I tried to tell Big Steve, but he accused me of making up stories to cover my butt."

After my conversation with Todd, any doubts I had about my wipeout being an act of sabotage evaporated— unlike the ice the saboteur had planted under the snow!

It may not have been the smoking gun that solved the case, but if it was true, it hit the bull's-eye when it came to proving a crime had been committed. But Todd hadn't told me anything that directly implicated Marni, and I wasn't any closer to figuring out why she'd done it—*if* she had done it.

It was time to expand my search and check out the saboteur's predawn route to set the trap on Round Top.

The ski-chair Liz and Brady had rigged for me was awesome, but it could only take me so far. To really explore the grounds and the backcountry, I was going to need something with more horsepower. . . .

Like a horse-drawn sleigh! I'd been watching guests ride them around the grounds all week and figured it was about time I got my turn too. A horse-drawn sleigh still might not be able to follow the trail all the way up the mountain itself, but the perp had to start at the bottom, and I could go there. There hadn't been any new snow and the wind had been calm, so there was a good chance I might be able to find tracks and other evidence. The last time I'd followed someone's tracks through the snow, I discovered a secret door!

Joe was headed up from town to meet me at noon, which was in about an hour. I thought about waiting for him, but I was antsy to get going. It was a winter wonderland out there! I told Henry to call me the next sleigh and to let Joe know I'd be back soon in case he arrived while I was gone.

The horse's sleigh bells weren't the only ones jingling when the sleigh pulled up in front of the lodge to pick me up.

"Ahoy, Miss Drew!" Jackie called from the driver's seat, using the reins to signal the gorgeous brown horse to stop. "Your one-horse open sleigh ride awaits! Just like the song!"

"Hi, Jackie!" I called back.

"It's a one-horse open sleigh and two broken legs!" proclaimed Henry, who'd accompanied me outside when we saw the sleigh coming.

"We can write our own verse!" Jackie said, giving her walking boot a jingle.

"You really do a little bit of everything around here," I noted.

"They don't call me Jackie-of-All-Trades for nothing!" she said. "Meet Clyde. He's our trustiest Clydesdale! Clyde and I will be leading your tour of the grounds, right, Clyde?"

"Nice to meet ya, Clyde," I said, grinning. Jackie's perky mood was contagious!

"What's that, Clyde?" Jackie said to the horse, leaning in like he was whispering to her. "Oh, I agree, Clyde. Miss Drew should be inside following doctor's orders and getting rest with that broken leg of hers."

"Thanks for your concern, Jackie, but I feel okay, really. It barely even hurts!" I assured her. "And besides, I'm going to go nuts if I'm stuck inside one more day. It's not the same looking at all this beauty out of a window."

"Well, I can tell Miss Drew is just about as stubborn as I am, so no use arguing, Clyde," she said to the horse, then turned back to me. "Hop on in, Miss Drew!"

"One hop coming up!" Henry announced, lifting

my broken leg and me gently into the front seat of the sleigh. There was just enough room up there to accommodate Jackie, me, and my cast.

"Have a nice ride!" Henry yelled out as we pulled away from the resort.

It felt so good to be outside pulled around in a sleigh, I almost forgot why I was there. It was Jackie who reminded me.

"So I hear you're the one who cracked the case," she whispered confidentially, even though there was no one else around.

I hadn't been broadcasting my investigation, but it also wasn't a secret, so it wasn't surprising that someone who wore as many hats at the lodge (and who liked to gossip as much!) as Jackie did would have gotten wind of it.

"No one could believe it when we heard it was Marni," she said, shaking her head in disbelief. "What a sweet girl. Everyone is as shocked as could be. Hopefully things will finally return to normal around here, though!"

"I hope so," I said, though I probably didn't sound entirely convincing.

"Here I am rambling when I'm supposed to be tour-guiding!" Jackie cheerily reprimanded herself. "So what would you like to see on your tour? The hot springs are always a guest favorite."

"Actually, I was wondering if we could take in some of the backcountry around where Round Top is," I suggested. I wasn't trying to hide anything from Jackie, but sharing details about an active case with someone who likes to gossip usually isn't the best way to keep secrets secret.

"Ooh, you're still investigating!" Jackie exclaimed. "Can I help?"

So much for subtlety.

"Um, sure," I conceded reluctantly, then tapped my cast. "Just driving me around to see Round Top is a huge help. It's hard for me to do much exploring on my own."

"Okay, I'm the detective's coach driver like in the old-timey Sherlock Holmes mysteries!" she proclaimed. "This is going to be so much fun!"

"Yeah, I think it will be," I said, and really meant it. It was hard not to have fun with Jackie around, and it definitely helped lighten the mood of the crime. I still was on vacation, after all.

"So what are we investigating anyway?" Jackie asked. "I thought the case was closed."

"Maybe," I said. "It's always good to be thorough and see if there's anything you missed."

"Hmm, you sound like a workaholic to me," she observed. "Why not just relax and enjoy the rest of your stay instead? Not that I have anything against work! I sure do enough of it! But you are still recuperating, and I can't help being a bit of a mother hen."

"Thanks for worrying about me, Jackie," I said. "It's really sweet, but I think I can do a little work and relax at the same time too! And you and Clyde are the ones doing all the hard work. It's not like sitting in a sleigh and taking in the scenery is exactly strenuous."

"All righty, have it your way, Detective McWorky-Pants, but I am going to take you the long way around so you can at least see some more of the scenery while you're here," she compromised. "We have plenty of daylight, and there's nothing quite so peaceful as a sleigh ride around our little mountaintop retreat."

"You win." I chuckled. I could tell arguing with Jackie wasn't going to get me anywhere, so I sat back and let her lead the way. It really was beautiful, and a little detour wouldn't hurt. "The hot springs it is."

You could see the steam rising from the springs at the far end of the frozen lake. The horse trail ran along the lake, with the water on one side and fluffy, snow-covered pine trees on the other. Mist began to settle over the trail as we neared the springs.

It would have been perfectly serene if it weren't for the faint growl of a motor somewhere up ahead.

"Do you hear that?" I asked Jackie.

Jackie cocked her head and listened as the noise grew louder. "Well, shoot, it sounds like those darn snowmobiles again. Nothing like a little noise pollution to poo on a perfectly pretty sleigh ride."

"Do they belong to the lodge?" I asked.

"Nah, we just got brand-new all-electric ones; you can barely hear them, they're so quiet," she said, narrowing her eyes in very un-Jackie-like fashion as the motor's obnoxious roar grew closer. "I'm guessing that's Dino and his hooligan friends again. They think it's cute to make a lot of noise and tear up the backcountry. We've reported it to the police a bunch of times, but Sheriff Pruitt seems to think it's funny."

I narrowed my eyes as well. George had said Pruitt had a bad habit of covering for Dino's petty crimes around town. I couldn't help wondering again if he might be covering for bigger crimes as well.

"It sounds like there are two snowmobiles, one ahead of us and one behind us," I noted as a second motor whirred into earshot from the backcountry beyond the horse trail.

"Whoa, Clyde!" Jackie said, pulling back on the reins. "I don't want to ride ahead into this mist not being able to see where Clyde is going. Those stupid machines might spook him, or worse, run into him!"

"Do we have to turn back?" I asked.

"Not yet. I'm going to walk ahead a bit and see who's out there first," said Jackie, handing me the reins.

"Um, what am I supposed to do with these?" I asked tentatively. "I've never driven a sleigh before."

"You're not driving, you're parking!" Jackie said with a wink. "Just hold on nice and tight. He shouldn't go anywhere unless you tell him to. Right, Clyde?"

Clyde neighed yes. At least that's what I hoped he meant!

"Are you going to be okay walking through the snow with your foot?" I asked.

"That's what this is for!" Jackie said, pulling a plastic grocery bag from her jacket pocket, shaking it open, and slipping it over her walking boot. "Keeps my boot dry. Recycling at its finest! I might not be able to sneak around on anybody with my fancy footwear on, but I can hobble along this horse trail just fine." She grabbed her cane and lowered herself off the sleigh, jingling as she went. "The mist starts to clear a little ways ahead. Just gonna take a quick peek to make sure the coast is clear, and then we'll be back on our merry way."

Jackie took a few jingly steps and vanished eerily into the mist. If it weren't for the sound of her sleigh bells fading down the path as she walked, it would have been like she was swallowed up entirely. I shuddered. The mist rising off the hot springs and settling over the snow-covered trail was beautiful *and* creepy.

And weirdly quiet all of a sudden. The whir of the snowmobiles had vanished as well, leaving Clyde and me in total creepy silence. My sleigh ride was starting to feel less like a winter wonderland Christmas card picture and more like a scene from a horror movie. Clyde seemed to think so too. He snorted and began shuffling his hooves nervously.

"Easy, boy, Jackie will be back in a minute," I reassured him, hoping it was true. I don't think I would have been so spooked, but the double whammy of the horror-movie mist and being trapped in my seat by a ginormo cast had me feeling uncomfortably claustrophobic. Not that I really thought I was going to have to run anywhere. At least I hoped not.

There was a sudden *THWACK* behind me, and a small jolt vibrated through the sleigh as if a stone had struck it, causing both Clyde and me to jump.

"Whoa, boy," I said, holding tight on the reins as Clyde whinnied and danced in place.

I cautiously looked behind me. I couldn't see anything except for trail and mist. The mist wasn't as dense behind us, but I couldn't be sure someone wasn't lurking off to the side of the trail.

Clyde whinnied again, pulling my attention back to the trail ahead of us, where a silhouetted figure began to emerge from the mist.

And it wasn't jingling.

"Jackie?" I croaked, but my voice came out as a whisper.

The figure stepped closer, its silhouette sharpening, the object in its hand becoming clearer. Jackie's cane pierced the mist and she stepped back into view.

I breathed a deep sigh of relief. "Jackie! Why aren't you jingling? You nearly scared me half to death!"

"Oops, sorry about that!" she said, stopping to give a perplexed glance down at her boot. "Silly thing keeps falling off. Don't worry, though, I've got extras!"

"Was there anyone out there?" I asked nervously.

"Didn't see a thing, just a bunch of churned-up snow," she said. "They must have moved on to make a mess somewhere else."

"I think someone might have thrown a rock at us while you were gone," I filled her in. "Clyde started to spook, and then something hit the sleigh."

Jackie's eyes went wide with concern. "If someone tried to hurt my Clyde, why, I'd . . ."

She trailed off as a motor roared to life on the trail behind us.

Clyde neighed loudly, dancing in place again. I turned around to see the lights of a snowmobile cutting through the fog, growing closer at an alarming pace as they raced right at us.

"Don't let go of the reins!" Jackie yelled, rushing toward us, ignoring her broken foot.

I had just tightened my grip on the reins when the

earsplitting *BOOM* of a gunshot exploded into the air behind us. Jackie tried to grab Clyde's bridle, but the terrified horse reared up on his hind legs, knocking her backward into the snow.

Then he took off, bolting down the trail with me alone in the sleigh, clinging desperately to his reins as the snowmobile roared closer.

CHAPTER EIGHTEEN

Screaming All the Way

CLYDE BROKE INTO A PANICKED GALLOP, slamming me back against my seat. The mist swallowed us a moment later. I could barely see my hands gripping Clyde's reins. I could sure feel them, though. I was holding on so tightly, I could feel the leather cut into my palms even through my thick ski mittens.

One-horse open sleighs don't come with seat belts, and if it weren't for my death grip on the reins, I would have gone flying right over the side. As it was, I was bouncing around like crazy, jolts of pain shooting through my ankle every time my cast banged against the seat.

"Doc Sherman isn't going to be happy about this!" I moaned as the snowmobile roared ever closer, spurring Clyde to gallop even faster. Poor, terrified Clyde! That huge Clydesdale heart of his must be pounding!

He veered off the trail, flashing past a warning sign of some sort, but we were moving so fast and there was so much mist, I saw only one word clearly: DANGER.

"That can't be good!" I cried.

Clyde burst through the mist into a snowy clearing at the base of a steep, snow-packed rocky slope with a jagged peak looming menacingly overhead.

And we weren't alone. A second snowmobile was waiting for us to emerge not far ahead. Its engine roared to life the second the driver saw us. It was an ambush! The snowmobile behind us had intentionally chased us right at its buddy.

I hadn't seen who was riding the snowmobile still pursuing us from behind, but the rider in front of us was dressed entirely in white with a full-faced ski mask, camouflaging them against the snow. The only thing I could tell about the rider was that they looked big. And they were rocketing right at us.

Clyde reared up in a spray of snow and cut hard left to get away from them, turning so suddenly the sleigh went airborne, swinging around behind him as it struggled to keep up. I cried out in pain as my cast jammed against the bench, but my awful, enormous cast wedging me into the seat was the only thing keeping me from tumbling out! The ridiculous thing had actually saved my life! The sleigh slammed back to the ground, somehow managing to stay upright as Clyde took off parallel to the snowy mountain peak on our right.

Another gunshot rang out behind us, reverberating through the cold mountain air. It was nothing compared to the deafening *WHUMP* that quickly followed from the peak rising over the clearing. It was immediately followed by a thundering rumble that dwarfed the sound of the snowmobiles' engines. I knew what it was before I saw the massive slab of packed snow start sliding off the mountain.

"Avalanche!" I screamed.

Clyde must have known it too, because he started galloping even faster, which I hadn't thought was possible. But even at a full gallop, a terrified horse can't outrace an avalanche. There were a million tons of runaway snow headed right at us, and the only thing we had going for us was a head start. We were racing parallel to the mountain—if Clyde could make it to the other side of the avalanche's path before the snow reached us, we might have a chance.

"Run, Clyde, run!" I yelled.

I don't know if it helped, but yelling encouragement was about the only thing I could do besides hanging on to his reins for dear life and hoping the sleigh didn't tip over. The ground shook beneath us, the wall of snow roaring toward us like a massive, endlessly crashing white wave.

By now, I had a pretty good hunch that the DANGER sign I'd seen flash by earlier had also included the word AVALANCHE. Whoever had chased us off the trail couldn't have been very smart, or they wouldn't have been firing a gun under a steep snow-packed slope.

Our pursuers might not have been geniuses, but they did have better escape vehicles.

I could see the second snowmobile propelling itself to safety with its high-horsepower engine. My escape vehicle may have only had a horsepower of one, but that one horse had heart!

"I believe in you, Clyde!" I screamed over the roar of the avalanche.

But the wall of snow kept closing in until it was towering over us. A cloud of cold whiteness engulfed me, snow slapping me in the face like an icy hand. It was too late! It . . .

"Whoo-hoo!" I shouted as Clyde yanked the sleigh through the bottom of the avalanche's path an instant before it swept past, showering us with so much snow it really did feel like riding through a cloud.

"Way to go, Clyde!" I cheered. "Way to . . . uh-oh . . ."

We were headed straight for the lake!

"Whoa!" I yelled, pulling back on the reins as hard as I could. It was no use, though. Clyde was out of control!

The lake may have been frozen enough for people to skate on, but a Clydesdale weighs over two thousand pounds! And that's without the sleigh. Or me. And as if things weren't bad enough, we were near the hot springs, where the ice would be the weakest from the heat.

The ice groaned under Clyde's weight, my sleigh skidding wildly behind him like a giant out-of-control ice skate. And then it cracked. The sound wasn't nearly as loud as the *WHUMP* of the avalanche, but it was just as frightening. I could see a huge, jagged crack shooting down the center of the ice in front of Clyde, and I could feel the ice falling apart under the sleigh's runners until there was icy water splashing up around us and I was practically water-skiing!

We'd gone from trying to outrun a giant slab of snow to trying to outrun a crumbling sheet of lake ice! Talk about going from the frying pan into the fire. This was like going from a carbonite cube into the cryogenic freezer!

"Head for the shore, Clyde!" I begged at the top of my lungs. "Please!"

Ice-skaters scattered. Snow geese skedaddled. Clyde kept galloping full speed ahead toward shore. We were almost there.

Only there was a bench in the way.

"Who puts a bench on a frozen lake?!" I shouted.

Clyde leaped over it. The sleigh didn't. The horse's reins were yanked from my hands as Clyde tore free from the sleigh's rigging and I went flying.

Landing face-first in a pile of snow never felt so good. I was cold, banged, and bruised, my ankle was throbbing, and my heart was beating a hundred miles an hour, but I was on solid land, and more importantly, I was alive!

I'd landed on the shore and the sleigh had crashed on its side a few feet away. I finally saw what had thwacked into it when I was waiting for Jackie to come back before the snowmobile started chasing us. It wasn't a rock. Someone had shot it with a crossbow. The bolt jutted from the wooden sleigh's side. Attached to it was a note:

BACK OFF.
OR ELSE.

CHAPTER NINETEEN

Trapped

MY SECOND RESCUE TOBOGGAN RIDE OF the trip arrived a few minutes later.

"We're going to have to get you a frequent-flier card, Nancy," Berkley, who picked me up (again!), joked to lighten the mood as he and a bearded ski patrolman I didn't know lifted me onto the toboggan. They weren't alone, though.

"You okay, Drew?" Joe asked, a look of deep concern on his face.

It seemed that my detecting partner was back from

his own mission. I was happy to see him; we had a lot to catch up on.

"A little shaken up, but it sure is good to see some friendly faces," I told them. "Are Clyde and Jackie okay?"

"Clyde's fine, just a little frightened," Berkley said. "Jackie got a toboggan ride of her own after some guests found her stumbling along the horse trail with a nasty gash on her head from Clyde knocking her over."

"She was a little woozy, but she told us about the snowmobiles shooting at you guys," Joe added.

"She was more worried about you and Clyde than anything," Berkley chimed in. "She's known ol' Clyde since he was a newborn colt."

"And half the lodge saw you coming across the lake!" Joe exclaimed. "Now *that* looked like fun."

"Next time you can take my place," I offered.

"I don't know about fun, but it sure does sound like you guys had a gnarly adventure," Berkley commented as he and his partner started to pull me back to the lodge.

"Yeah, and it may not be over," I said softly, making sure Berkley and his partner weren't looking before locking eyes with Joe and nodding at the note pinned to the sleigh's side. Joe gritted his teeth.

"We've got some work to do after you see the doc, Drew," he said, hanging back to take a cell phone pic and carefully remove the crossbow bolt and the note to preserve the evidence. It's exactly what I would have done if I hadn't been strapped to a toboggan in a humungous cast.

I didn't know who it was, but someone was trying to scare me off the case. If they thought I could be scared off that easily, then they didn't know Nancy Drew. Okay, maybe I was a little scared—maybe I was super, ridiculously, terrifyingly scared. But not so scared that I'd let it stop me from investigating. No way. If anything, I was even more determined. There's nothing wrong with being frightened—detecting can be a frightening business, just as long as it doesn't stop you from doing what's right.

"Have the police and the state troopers been called?"

I asked, ready to get right back to business. "The avalanche would have buried some of it, but those snowmobilers may have left shell casings and other evidence behind."

"They've been called, but it's not going to do much good," Joe replied.

"That avalanche triggered a second avalanche farther down the mountain that took out the road to the lodge," Berkley explained.

"I got here just before it happened," Joe said. "Otherwise I'd still be stuck back in Prospect."

"And now you're stuck here. No cars are coming in or out of here until the road is cleared, and with the blizzard that's supposed to hit us tonight, that could be a couple days at least." Berkley sighed. "Looks like we might all be spending Christmas Eve snowed in here instead of home with our families."

Doc Sherman may not have been any nicer or more talkative than the first time I saw him, but his boil must have been feeling a little better, because he did seem concerned at least. Everyone at the lodge was rattled by what had happened, and it seemed to have the doc even jumpier and lip-chewier than he had been the first time I saw him. You'd almost think he'd been the one on the runaway sleigh. I guess it's not every day a ski resort physician has to treat people after their horse-drawn sleigh is chased through an avalanche and across a frozen lake by gun-wielding bad guys on snowmobiles. One of us could easily have been killed.

"Is Jackie doing okay?" I asked. The nurse, Mariana, had told me on the way in that Jackie had a mild concussion and needed stitches for the gash on her head. I didn't want to think how much worse it could have been if two-thousand-pound Clyde had accidentally stomped her or if she'd gotten caught under the sleigh—or run over by the snowmobile!—after Clyde knocked her down.

"Jackie is resting, which is exactly what you should have been doing," he scolded. "None of this would have happened if you had stayed in bed like you were supposed to."

"I . . . I'm sorry," I said, swallowing the impulse to defend myself. Both Jackie and Doc Sherman had worked at the lodge for a long time, and it had to be hard for a doctor to treat someone they knew after a near miss like that. Besides, even though getting chased by snowmobile thugs *definitely* wasn't my fault, it was technically true that they wouldn't have tried to warn me off the case if I hadn't been investigating in the first place.

"Mariana will take you for X-rays," he said, turning to leave the room.

It wasn't until I glanced up and noticed the calendar on the exam room wall that I remembered—tomorrow was supposed to be the day I got my cast off! It seemed a little soon to me, but I figured Dr. Sherman knew what he was doing.

"Wait a second, Doc!" I called after him. "I still get my cast off tomorrow morning, right?"

He glared at me for a minute before replying. "That will depend on the X-rays."

He was gnawing on his lip especially hard a half

~ 269 ~

hour later when he came back into the exam room and laid the new X-rays on the desk.

"You're making me a little nervous, Doc," I told him. From the look on his face, you'd think I had only a few hours left to live.

"Your lower leg is badly swollen, and the healing of your tibia is almost certainly set back. And the fracture is nowhere near healed," he began, and my heart sank. He sounded as severe as he had after my first set of X-rays came back. "But there are no further breaks . . . miraculously," he concluded, shaking his head in amazement.

"That's great news!" I exclaimed. "So the cast can come off and I can get a boot!"

"No," he said bluntly.

"But you said after seven days if—" I started to plead my case, but he cut me off before I could finish.

"You could have been killed," he snapped in a tone that sounded somewhere between an accusation and genuine concern. "I'm not taking any chances after the ordeal you've been through. I want your leg to remain immobilized until the swelling goes down and I can be sure there isn't any additional trauma."

I must have had a serious puppy-dog pout going, because his voice softened.

"None of us are going anywhere for the next day or two until the road is clear anyway, so you can come back and see me then," he said apologetically. "Just please stay off it this time. *Please.*"

I didn't want to lie to him, so I just smiled reassuringly.

I had to smile reassuringly at Archie, too, later that afternoon.

"Absolutely no more investigating," he implored. "I'd rather lose the lodge than someone's life."

"What did Grant say?" I asked without exactly replying.

"He . . . What he said isn't your concern anymore, Nancy," Archie said, cutting his original thought short. "But to put your mind at ease, he says it's his campaign manager who recommended the All Alloy stock and took the funds from that Crane guy you mentioned.

Grant swears he didn't know anything about the oil connections, and now that he does, he's looking for a replacement to run his next campaign."

"Hmm . . . ," I said noncommittally. "What are you going to do about the pipeline?"

"I . . . I don't want you to worry about it," he sighed. "I've involved you in the lodge's problems too many times already, and it's nearly gotten you killed. Right now, all I want is to get through the next couple days. We've got nearly our entire staff and a quarter of our rooms stuck here with a major storm coming and no way for anyone to leave the grounds, let alone get home by tomorrow night in time for the holiday."

"Is there anything I can do to help?" I offered.

"You can help by staying out of harm's way until I can get you and everyone else off the mountain and home safely," he said, looking forlornly up at the lobby speakers as they began to play "I'll Be Home for Christmas."

Then he walked away, grumbling to himself. "A merry Christmas, indeed."

. . .

The sound of tiny sleigh bells jingling perked up my holiday spirit. I wheeled myself around the corner, expecting to see Jackie, but found Liz and the kids instead.

"You're jingling just like Jackie!" I told Kelly, who had a set of Jackie's tiny sleigh bells dangling from the pom-pom on top of her ski hat.

"I found them in the reading room when we were testing out the moving staircase," Kelly said, giving her head a jingly shake.

Liz rolled her eyes. "I leave the room for two seconds and Brady lets them climb that thing. I come back and Kelly is throwing those little bells down at the other Things."

I had to laugh at the image. "Sounds like a fun afternoon!"

"We were just on our way to leave them at the front desk for Jackie when she's feeling better," Liz said.

"Jackie has extras. I'm sure she wouldn't mind if Kelly held on to this one," I suggested.

"Yeah, finders keepers!" Kelly said.

"That's exactly why we're going to give it back," Liz asserted, looking at Kelly and holding out her open palm. "What I told you guys about sharing the slopes with other skiers goes for real life too. You can ask Jackie if she wants to share them next time we see her."

"Fine," Kelly relented, dropping the bells in Liz's hand.

"So what's the latest on the investigation?" Liz asked.

"The latest on the investigation is everyone seems to want me to stop investigating," I huffed.

Liz gave me a knowing smile. "Well, if you need any help *not* investigating, just give Brady and me a shout. We'll be outside playing in the snow. I love me a good blizzard!"

"We're going to build a whole army of snowmen!" Jimmy said.

"And snow-women!" Grace insisted.

"And snow vampires with capes!" Kelly added. "Like the ones that shape-shift into bats in that creepy book Brady read to us in the library room."

"I told Brady not to read *Dracula* to them," she lamented. "He had nightmares all night."

"The reading room . . . ," I muttered to myself, barely registering what Liz said. "Shape-shifting . . ."

"You okay, Nancy?" Liz asked. "You look like you're in some kind of detective trance or something."

"Better than okay! Thank you, Kelly!" I said, grabbing her and kissing her on the top of the head. "I've got to go!"

Joe and I stood in the second-floor reading room, staring at the built-in shelves lining the walls. Well, Joe stood, at least. I sat, if you want to get technical about it.

"And you think there's a secret door here why?" Joe asked.

"Kelly mentioned the reading room and shapeshifting and it suddenly came to me: the secret door in Chef K's pantry is hidden by original built-in shelves just like these," I explained. "The burglar has been sneaking in and out of rooms unseen without tampering with the locks, and if there are other shape-shifting secret doors, the reading rooms could be central access points that let them do it."

"Huh. There are other common rooms with the same kind of old built-in shelves too, though," Joe pointed out. "Couldn't there be secret doors there as well?"

"You're right, there totally could be!" I said, pondering the possibility of secret passages all over the lodge like Mrs. Bosley hoped. There was a catch, though. "All the other built-in shelves like these I've seen are on the ground floor in the lobby or the lounge, and other high-traffic areas."

"So even if there were secret doors, they'd be a lot harder for a perp to access without being seen," Joe extrapolated.

"Yup. The people who use this reading room are mostly the guests on this floor, and I've only seen a few people in here the whole week," I said. "And I felt a strange draft." I wheeled myself over to the corner of the wall with the fireplace. "Right about here."

There it was again, tickling my toes at the sock-covered tip of my cast.

"Okay, so if there is a secret door, how do we unlock it?" Joe asked.

"I don't know," I admitted. "But we might not have to. Chef K said hers only opens from the inside, as far as she can tell, so she leaves the mechanism unlatched and cracks the door a hair to keep it from locking when she wants to use it from the other side. Maybe our perp does the same."

"So, what, I just pull?" Joe asked skeptically, grabbing hold of a shelf.

"Maybe?" I suggested.

He tried yanking on the shelf, but it was hard to get a grip and nothing budged except a couple of old clothbound Tom Swift adventure novels.

"Nada," he said. "Even if it was unlocked, the wall's too heavy and I don't have any leverage."

"Maybe we need to take this to the next level," I said, eyeing the rolling staircase that had been serving as a jungle gym for Things One through Three earlier in the afternoon. It had been pushed all the way to the other side of the room. "If you wheel that staircase over, you might be able to get more leverage."

"Swift thinking, Drew," Joe said.

He wheeled it over and gave the shelf a strong yank.

"Bingo!" he exclaimed as the shelf-lined wall creaked open just wide enough for a person to slip through.

I quickly wheeled over and peered in as best I could from my chair. Joe flicked on the little LED flashlight he had hanging from his key chain and aimed it into a dark, narrow passage.

Joe's light was only powerful enough to illuminate a few feet of dirt floor and cobweb-lined old plank walls. The only way we'd find out what lay beyond was to step inside.

"I hate to turn down a secret passage that might be filled with gold, but it looks like you're going in alone," I lamented, flicking the wheel of my chair. "Keep within earshot, and I'll keep watch. If you hear me talking to anyone, stay put till I give you the all clear."

"I feel weird going through a secret door without my bro here to annoy me, but you're a pretty good substitute, Drew," said Joe, grinning, as he slipped inside the secret passage, using his flashlight to light the way.

He pulled the hidden door partially closed behind him and vanished into the darkness.

A few minutes later he emerged, a lot dustier, but still in one piece.

"I didn't find any gold, but I did find this," Joe said, and stepped back into the reading room holding a long, braided lock of dark brown clip-on hair that looked just like Marni's trademark braid.

CHAPTER TWENTY

Really Trapped!

"MARNI WAS FRAMED!" I EXCLAIMED, FILLED with relief that my instincts about her had been right.

"The braid was snagged under the inside of the door, so I'm guessing the perp accidentally dropped it," Joe told me. "I wouldn't have seen it if my light hadn't randomly reflected off the clip."

"Whoever sabotaged the trail to take out Chef K must've thrown on a ski patrol uniform and clipped that on to make it look like Marni if they were spotted," I deduced, taking the braid from Joe and examining it.

The braid was made of natural fiber, but it was a lot

coarser than human hair and definitely seemed home-made rather than store-bought. "It might not look real up close, but you'd never be able to tell from a distance."

"The fake braid isn't the only thing I found in the passage," Joe said ominously. "There's another one of those old animal traps your friend almost stepped in, and this one still has its teeth."

"The passage is booby-trapped," I said, cringing at the thought of the cruel iron trap.

"Yup," Joe confirmed. "It's hard to tell with a small flashlight and all that dust, but I think there are also trip wires a few yards farther down the passage in each direction before it seems to dead-end on both sides."

"Are they dead ends?" I wondered. "Or more trap-doors?"

"Trapdoors would be my guess," Joe agreed. "But I wasn't about to stumble through a gauntlet of animal traps and trip wires to find out where they led."

I gave a cautious look back at the reading room's entrance. "Let's put the shelves back where they were and break the clues down somewhere else. The perp could be practically anyone, and we don't want to get spotted hanging out in front of their secret lair."

"Well, you were right about the secret passage," Joe said once we were safely back in my suite.

There was a steady, heavy snow falling out the window, and according to the latest forecast, it was supposed to keep up like this for hours.

"There could be a whole network of passages," I replied. "I'm betting Grant's suite has built-in shelves with a hidden door too. It would definitely explain how the perp has been able to sneak in and out of rooms so easily."

I was tempted to call Henry or Archie and ask them, but at this point I wasn't sure who I could trust other than Joe—whoever had been using the secret passage to break into rooms had been doing it well before the Hardy Boys arrived in town.

"Speaking of the perp," I continued, "they knew there was no way for anyone to see their face if they were spotted moving the trail signs. Anyone of roughly average size could have worn the braid and pulled off the disguise from that far away."

"If they were average size, we know it wasn't Sheriff Pruitt," Joe said, sounding disappointed. "That's a large dude."

"Or Dino Bosley, but that doesn't mean it wasn't one of their accomplices," I said. "We know at least two people were involved in the snowmobile ambush. The second one looked pretty big, but the first one could have been Frosty the Snowman or one of Santa's elves for all I know. I only saw their headlights."

"So what do we know for sure?" Joe asked.

"That the case didn't end with Marni's arrest," I said. "And that we have the evidence to free her from jail."

"But if we do, the perps will for sure know we're onto them," Joe pointed out.

"And where to find us," I said, shuddering. "With the road closed by the avalanche, we're practically sitting ducks."

"Well, technically, you're a Sitting Drew," Joe remarked.

"So we're basically trapped in the lodge with at least one and possibly multiple violent criminals on the loose and no way for anyone to reach us," I summarized.

"That sounds about right," Joe confirmed.

"Well, I guess there's nothing left to do but catch the crooks," I said.

"Sounds good to me," replied Joe. "The only problem is we aren't any closer to discovering who's been using the secret passages or why."

I looked out at the snow piling up atop the maze's intricately pruned hedges and thought about the animal trap the perp had left behind in the secret reading-room door. Extreme circumstances sometimes call for extreme measures.

"Are you up for a little subterfuge?" I asked Joe.

"Hit me with it, Drew," he said.

"We'll set a trap of our own to lure the perp out of hiding," I declared. "How warm are your clothes?"

"I've got a bunch of good cold-weather gear in the car," he said. "I could camp out in the snow overnight and be perfectly toasty."

"Good," I said, pointing to the Grand Sky Lodge notepad on the table. "Hand me that pad."

> *I know what you did. So will everyone*
> *else if you don't come to the maze at 11:30*
> *tonight with enough of that gold you gave*
> *the waiter to buy my silence. Start at the*
> *maze lower gate, take two lefts, a right,*
> *and a left. Come alone. No disguises. No*
> *funny business.*
> —*Your Secret Santa*

"I like it!" Joe exclaimed after he read the note I'd written on the notepad, using my left hand to disguise my handwriting. "We flip the script on the anonymous note-leaver who paid off Clark and leave them an anonymous note instead."

"We leave this inside the reading-room secret passage somewhere they can't miss it, and then you hide inside the maze to get an ID on whoever shows up," I said, filling him in on my plan.

"And then I jump out, tie them up, and drag them back to the lodge!" Joe offered excitedly.

"No!" I said quickly. "We just want them to reveal themselves! All you need to do is hide and identify them. Whoever is doing this is mondo dangerous, and you won't have any backup. The people who chased me earlier today weren't shy about using guns."

"Meaning they could just try to silence me with lead instead of gold," Joe said, catching on.

"We'll let them think you're a no-show, and then you can sneak back out through a different gate after they leave," I said.

"Fine, no heroic subduing of the bad guy," he sulked.

"If they do spot you, you can slip away into the maze, where it will be hard for them to follow without getting lost themselves," I said.

"But how do I keep from getting lost in the maze?" asked Joe.

"Easy," I said, looking out over the maze below. Even with the steady snowfall, the holiday lights strung over the tops of the hedges illuminated the whole pattern clearly. "We map out all the turns to get you just within view of the directions I left on the note—if I'm right, it should be the perfect hiding spot for you to spy on them without being seen. I can also use my binoculars to guide you over the radio. I may not be able to see you on the ground once you're inside the hedges, but if you do get lost, you can turn on the blinker on your LED light, and I should be able to spot you from above that way."

"How do we know they'll even show?" Joe asked. "They may not use the secret passage again until later."

"We don't," I said. "It's a gamble. But do you have anything better to do tonight?"

"Good point," he conceded. "Let's do this!"

"There's one call I have to make first," I said, thinking about Bess and the can of pepper spray she always carries for self-defense. Someone had already tried to take me out once that day, and alone in my room with my cast on, I really was a Sitting Drew. If anyone tried to get in, I wanted to be prepared. I might not have access to store-bought cans of chemical Mace like Bess kept in her purse, but I did know someone with plenty of organic ammunition we could use to concoct our own variation.

"Hey, Chef," I said when she answered her cell phone. "I need a quick favor."

It didn't take long for Chef K to whip me up a cup full of habanero powder, and for Joe to rig it over my suite door with fishing line running across the living room to my wheelchair. If anyone tried breaking in through the door while Joe was on his mission, all I'd have to do was give it a yank and they'd get a face full of the same powerful powdered pepper that caused all that mayhem at the opening night banquet.

"There's a little bit left over in the coffee cup on the buffet table by the window," Joe said. "Don't mistake it for coffee and take a gulp."

"Good advice," I agreed, handing him the two-way radio I'd had Chef K send up with the hot pepper.

Joe left our bait note on the floor of the secret passage, weighted down by an electric candle so whoever entered the passage wouldn't miss it. He had navigated his way through the maze to the hiding spot and was lying in wait by ten forty-five p.m., just in case the perp decided to show up early and surprise him.

All I could do now was watch through my binoculars and wait. The waiting was the hardest part. It got even harder as the snow picked up—and it picked up fast! The hours of heavy, steady snow had suddenly turned into a full-on blizzard! Wind howled down off the mountain, billowing the snow off the ground in great clouds.

Joe would hopefully be sheltered from the worst of the wind by the maze's hedges, but the storm was quickly nearing whiteout conditions. Pretty soon I'd be helpless to guide him through the maze if he needed me to.

There was a flash of light off in the distance, followed by the unmistakable crack of thunder. This wasn't just any old snowstorm! I'd heard about "thundersnow" before, but it's such a rare meteorological event, I'd never actually seen it. It would have been really cool if it weren't happening right in the middle of our operation!

There was another flash of lightning, this one close enough that I could see the bolt pierce through the storm. The Grand Sky Lodge went dark before the sound of the thunderclap reached us. The only light in my suite now came from the electric fireplace. Outside, dim solar-powered emergency lights went on around the grounds, but the decorative holiday lights were entirely dark—including the ones over the maze. Between the power outage and the blizzard, Joe would be left practically in the dark!

I'm sure he's fine, I told myself. *If he thinks he's in trouble, he'll turn on his flashlight and I can try to guide him that way.*

I hadn't known Joe very long, but I got the impression he'd see hiding out in a thundersnow blizzard, waiting for a bad guy, as more of an adventure than a predicament.

Still, the chances of the perp venturing out in this storm were slim, and Joe's safety came first. If the storm got any worse, it would be hard for him to retrace his steps even with the directions.

It was time to call Joe in.

I had just picked up my walkie-talkie when I glimpsed more lights in the distance beyond the maze. Only these were coming from the ground, not the sky, and they seemed to be getting closer.

I lifted the binoculars and struggled to adjust the focus to see through the storm. The lights cutting through the snow *definitely* weren't lightning. They were headlights from two small vehicles. I might not have recognized what they were if I hadn't seen the lights just like them cut through the mist on the horse trail earlier that day.

Snowmobiles.

My two sleigh-ride saboteurs were back, and they were headed straight for Joe.

The headlights came to a stop down the hill from the maze and shut off, turning my binoculars' field of vision dark. But it was only dark for a moment. A jagged bolt of lightning pierced the sky, illuminating the silhouettes of two hulking figures carrying chain saws. A second later it was dark again.

I dropped the binoculars and grabbed the walkie-talkie.

"It's an ambush, Joe!" I whispered urgently into the walkie-talkie. "They're going to cut through the maze with chain saws! Get out of there now!"

Only there was no answer. Not even static this time. Just awful silence. My walkie-talkie battery wasn't working!

I pulled out my cell phone and frantically opened my call log to find Joe's number. I was about to press it when I saw the "No Service" icon on the top of the screen. The storm must have knocked out the cell towers along with the power.

My heart nearly beat out of my chest as I struggled to see anything through the curtain of snow. Our trap had been turned around on us and there was nothing I could do.

No, not nothing, I told myself.

I struggled out of my chair, ignoring the pain in my ankle as I stood up and unlocked the window. There was a loud creak as I yanked it open and yelled into the raging blizzard, hoping my voice would reach the maze over the storm.

"Run, Joe!" I screamed, my voice disappearing into the howling wind and snow.

Snow billowed in through the open window, causing me to shiver, but there was another draft of cool air I didn't expect, and this one was coming from behind me.

It suddenly occurred to me that the creaking I'd heard a moment before hadn't come from the window opening at all.

"Shut up and sit back down," a strangely familiar angry voice snarled behind me.

I turned around slowly. I wasn't alone in the suite anymore. A person in a ski mask stood in front of an open secret door in my room. The door had been concealed by the breakfast nook. So much for my precautions! That wasn't my only surprise, though.

The person had a shiny new ax gripped tightly in their fist.

CHAPTER TWENTY-ONE

The Grinch

SNOW BLEW IN THROUGH THE OPEN WINDOW, landing at my feet to remind me that Joe was still outside with chain-saw-wielding attackers bearing down on him. It was a double ambush!

"I said sit down," the masked intruder snarled again, and slammed the ax into the breakfast nook table.

"I'm only sitting down because I'm not used to standing and my ankle hurts," I said as I got into the wheelchair again. I wasn't going to give the intruder the satisfaction of thinking they could bully me.

"Get over here," he or she growled back through clenched teeth.

Where did I know that voice from? It was muffled by the face mask, making it harder to discern, but that made me realize it had also been muffled when I'd heard it before. Only last time it hadn't been by fabric. It had been by static. It was the same voice I'd heard screaming at someone over the radio when Bradley's channels got crossed on the slopes after I broke my leg!

Not that the revelation did me much good. It had sounded familiar that time too, and I hadn't been able to place it then, either. Figuring out where I knew the voice from didn't have me any closer to knowing who it belonged to.

If I could keep them talking, I might be able to figure it out.

"I think I'd rather stay where I am, thanks," I said, trying not to let the fear show in my voice.

The masked perp let out a cruel laugh and pulled the ax from the table. "Don't make me come get you."

I gulped. There was an even more pressing reason

to keep them talking than figuring out their identity: staying alive!

I'd taken precautions against someone trying to get at me while Joe was outside, but the intruder's surprise secret door had rendered those precautions useless. I glanced from the powder-filled coffee cup a few feet out of reach on the buffet table over to the suite door, where Joe had rigged the hot pepper trap. I had two last lines of defense; one of them was out of reach and the other was out of range. If I could somehow get the intruder to move under the door, I could pull the fishing line to unleash the trap.

"In case you hadn't noticed, my chair isn't going to fit through that passage," I pointed out.

The intruder grunted. Apparently they hadn't thought about that.

"We could just go out the door instead," I suggested, and began wheeling myself over, hoping they'd at least move toward the door to cut me off.

They didn't.

"Stop!" the person bellowed, slamming the ax

down again with so much force it cleaved a chunk of wood from the table.

I stopped.

"You'll walk," they growled.

"Not gonna happen," I replied.

"Then I'll drag you," they threatened. "Your choice."

I wanted to kick myself as I looked at the suite's doorknob, where the tiny sleigh bells Jackie had given me the day I broke my leg, so we could be twinsies, hung uselessly. I'd put them there to alert me if anyone tried to get in, but they didn't do much good against a burglar who didn't bother with doors—at least not ones you could see.

I'd been pretty proud of myself for figuring out that the lodge's built-in shelves hid concealed doors, but I'd made the mistake of assuming that was how the perp had snuck into Grant's suite and everywhere else. I hadn't been thinking about the other original built-in furniture the lodge also had. Like the benches and breakfast nooks. Too bad I hadn't hung one of Jackie's bells from there instead.

"That's it!" I blurted aloud, realizing that there was another place Jackie's bells *had* turned up that was equally unexpected. The ones little Kelly had found on the rolling staircase in the reading room. There was no way someone with a broken foot could have dropped them there.

"Stop jabbering, and get moving!" the intruder shouted. Only this time, it dawned on me why I hadn't been able to place the voice.

The person's voice was normally so chipper and cheery, it had seemed impossible to imagine it as anything else. The venom coming from the bad guy in front of me was totally out of character with the super-happy, jingly woman with the clumsy limp I thought I knew.

"The bells were a nice touch, Jackie," I said. "No one would ever suspect someone who limped around in a walking boot and jingled everywhere they went of sneaking all over the lodge, breaking into people's rooms and committing sabotage. It gave you the perfect alibi."

"It was pretty brilliant, wasn't it?" Jackie commented

as she pulled off the ski mask, revealing the fresh stitches in her forehead. "It's about time you figured it out. It was getting stuffy under that thing and making my stitches itch."

"Your foot wasn't really hurt, was it?" I asked.

"I think I would have made a decent actress, don't you?" she replied, giving the wall an enthusiastic kick with her supposedly broken foot. "They don't call me Jackie-of-All-Trades for nothin'."

"Pretending to be a nice person is a pretty rotten talent, if you ask me," I spat. I felt totally betrayed. I had genuinely liked Jackie and had been touched by how much she seemed to care about me getting enough rest—when in reality she was the one responsible for my broken leg the whole time.

"I *am* a nice person," she insisted. "As long as you don't mess with me. And you've turned into a royal bee in my bonnet. So let's get going before you get me really peeved."

"There's no way I'm just walking into that passage with you," I stated.

"It's a lot easier than the alternative," she said, tapping the ax against the table. "I might actually consider paying you off like your little note said if I had enough gold to spare and thought you'd actually take it."

"So Mrs. Bosley's gold rush treasure is real?" I asked, momentarily forgetting about my dire predicament.

"It's not Mrs. Bosley's," Jackie snapped. "She may have told everyone the legend, but I'm the one who found the hidden passages and the map."

"There's a map?" I asked. Even with Jackie threatening me with an ax, it was hard not to get excited about the legend being real.

"Part of one," she revealed. "I found it on a torn piece of parchment in one of the passages. I've only uncovered a couple of small pouches with a few nuggets so far, but I'm close to the mother lode, I know it! If you want to help me find the rest, I'd be happy to cut you in for a small percentage."

My brain was racing. Gold really was the motive, but I still had a million questions.

"What does your revenge campaign against Chef K have to do with the gold?" I asked, ignoring Jackie's attempt to bribe me. "She doesn't know anything about the treasure and couldn't care less. She thinks it's a ridiculous fairy tale. All she wants is to be left alone to cook."

"Oh, it's not revenge," Jackie said matter-of-factly. "She's just in my way. I tried to be nice. I even took her one of my famous fruitcakes as a welcome present when she first got here, but she kicked me right out of the restaurant, fruitcake and all!"

"You sabotaged the trail that broke my leg, spiked a banquet hall full of people with hot pepper, nearly lit the restaurant on fire with the menorah stunt, stunk up the entire lodge with rotten cabbage, set out animal traps, tried to send Chef K off a cliff, and framed Marni for it all because she turned down your fruitcake?!" I asked indignantly. "Someone's a little sensitive about their baking."

"I didn't do it because of the fruitcake, silly," Jackie said, her mood lightening. "She banned *everyone* from the restaurant. According to my map, there's a secret tunnel leading to an old gold mine behind the wall of the room the contractor uncovered during the renovation. If I'm not allowed near the kitchen, I can't get to the treasure."

"So there *is* another secret passage hidden behind the new pantry shelves Chef K put up!" I exclaimed. My hunch about the uncovered chamber hiding other secrets was right. "That's where you think the treasure is?"

Jackie just smiled. "Being sugary sweet usually opens all kinds of doors for me, but not that one. It's her own fault, really. Miss Fancy-Pants Chef is just too grumpy for her own good. I've been working here my whole life and she strolls in from the city one day and thinks she can hog the place all to herself. The nerve!"

"So you decided to take her out?" I surmised.

"You make it sound so sinister, dear," Jackie said. "But it sure would make getting into that room a lot easier if she wasn't around anymore. I had hoped to just pester her into leaving, but she's near as stubborn as you are! I'm afraid more drastic measures were necessary."

A lot of the edge had left Jackie's voice and she sounded almost chipper again. She actually seemed to be enjoying talking about her crimes, which wasn't too surprising, considering how much of a self-proclaimed talker she was. That worked for me. The longer I could keep her talking, the more time I bought myself.

"Why target Representative Alexander?" I asked. "Is there a connection between the gold and the pipeline?"

"The pipeline?" she replied. "Oh, how cute! The detective is confused! I'd be as happy as anyone else here if the pipeline took a hike, but I don't have anything to do with all that."

"Then what were you looking for in his room?" I asked.

"The same thing I was looking for in all the rooms," she said. "More secret doors with hidden passages that might give me another way into the tunnel behind the chef's pantry. Although I have to admit, it is kind of fun snooping into other people's secrets along the way. But I've searched the dickens out of the entire lodge and can't seem to find another way into the tunnel anywhere."

"Which explains why nothing was taken in any of the break-ins," I said to myself, fitting the pieces of the mystery together.

"And why our new chef guarding all her goodies like a tapas tyrant is such a problem," Jackie added, glancing at her watch. "Oh, where does the time go? Sometimes I get chatting and can hardly stop. The treasure isn't going to find itself, though! So what do you think about keeping all this our little secret and helping me get rid of Chef K so I can find the rest of the gold?"

I leveled with her. "I think this will go a lot easier for you if you come clean to the authorities now before your list of crimes gets any longer. If you try to kidnap me on top of everything else, you may spend the rest of your life behind bars."

"Didn't think so," Jackie sighed. "That's why you're going to have to come with me. Such a shame. I didn't want to hurt you, but it doesn't look like you're leaving me any choice."

"Didn't want to hurt me?" I shouted, pointing out the open window. "What do you call sending those two snowmobiles out there after me earlier today? Clyde and I barely survived!"

"I would never do anything to harm Clyde!" she shouted back, slamming the ax back into the table and pointing to the fresh stitches on her forehead, where she'd been cut when Clyde knocked her over. "Do you think I did this to myself?"

I gave her a hard stare and decided I believed her. I knew she really had been hurt from what Brady told me, and the stitches on her forehead confirmed that at least one of her injuries was real.

"I was just trying to keep tabs on you and give you the runaround to make sure you didn't get too close," she growled. "I don't have anything to do with those dreadful hooligans—well, at least not until I got your little extortion note I didn't."

Jackie's scowl turned back into a grin as she looked past me out the window. "I wondered if they might show back up."

"Call them off right now before someone gets hurt really badly," I urged. "It's not too late for you to put an end to this."

"I'm sorry, dear, calling them off isn't up to me. Why, I wouldn't even know how to reach them if I wanted to," she said. "And putting an end to it is exactly what I'm doing."

"If you didn't call them, who did?" I demanded.

"The fall guy I set up to take the blame for all that pesky sabotage around here would be my guess," she said cryptically. "But it sounds like he called in some friends to take his place. From what I heard you yelling to your friend, you both might disappear tonight, and then I guess all the bad guys will get away with it! Although taking him down in the process would have been a nice cherry on top of the fruitcake."

"Taking who down?" I insisted. I was getting fed up with Jackie's riddles. Joe was in danger, and I needed to figure out how to stop it.

"You see, I got your clever little invitation to the maze, but I figured if you really knew who you were leaving it for, you would have mentioned me by name," she reasoned. "So instead of taking your bait, I edited your invitation and left an anonymous version of my own for a certain someone else to find. Not much goes on around here that Jackie-of-All-Trades doesn't learn about, and it turns out I'm not the only person with something to hide."

"So when he, whoever "he" is, showed up in the maze in your place, Joe and I would assume he was the one responsible for the sabotage and the break-ins," I said, reconstructing how she'd turned our trap around on us. "When he'd really been sent by you to take the fall for your crimes."

"I know, it's just brilliant, isn't it?" she said, congratulating herself. "I knew he had a guilty conscience and would try to cover his tracks by either paying off the blackmailer, in which case you'd pin the crime on him . . ."

"Or he'd call their muscle back in to take us out of the picture," I finished Jackie's sentence for her, my stomach dropping as I thought about the chain-saw-wielding thugs stalking toward the maze.

"Either way, I'd be in the clear and could just lie low for a while," Jackie said.

"Only your not-so-perfect plan went sideways when little Kelly found your bells somewhere a person in a walking boot shouldn't have been able to go, and you got scared it might implicate you instead of the fall guy," I deduced.

"Those stupid bells keep getting lost in the most inconvenient places. I only found out about the ones in the reading room because Liz had Kelly ask me if she could keep them," Jackie lamented. "I wasn't worried about anyone else figuring it out, but you are the famous Nancy Drew after all. I knew if you got wind of it, you'd piece together that it was me eventually."

"So you revised your plan to take me out first while the setup you orchestrated was going on in the maze," I said.

"They say the best defense is a good offense," Jackie asserted.

The faint hum of distant chain-saw motors carried through the open window along with the sound of the storm. I turned around and looked down the hill. The whiteout-condition blizzard had lessened back to a heavy snowfall, but the storm was far from over for Joe and me. The thugs' flashlight beams formed snowy halos of light inside the darkened maze. If I didn't figure something out quickly, both Joe and I might be goners.

"All the fall guys in the world don't do me much good if you're still around to pin everything on me," Jackie said, stalking toward me with the ax. "Time to go, Miss Drew."

I grabbed the wheels of my chair, preparing to race for the table with the coffee cup full of habanero powder, when the tiny sleigh bells hanging from the knob of the suite door jingled.

We both turned as the door swung open and Doc Sherman stepped inside.

Jackie's eyes narrowed.

"It's about time you showed up," she snapped. "I'm always the one doing the hard work. Now help me get her back into the passage before someone else walks in."

CHAPTER TWENTY-TWO

~

Rear Window

THERE WAS A REASON DOC SHERMAN HAD been so jumpy every time he saw me. He was Jackie's accomplice. The same person who had put me in my cast had given Jackie her phony one.

He closed the door behind him and looked nervously from Jackie gripping her ax to me in my wheelchair to the snow blowing through the open window behind me.

"What kind of doctor helps someone hurt his patients?" I cried, ready to yank the fishing line connected to the booby trap over his head and shower him in hot pepper.

"Not a very good one," he said, blowing out his checks. "I'm sorry for what we've put you through, Nancy."

I lightened my touch on the fishing line.

"Help me grab her," Jackie commanded, but Doc Sherman didn't budge.

"No," he said quietly.

"What?!" Jackie raged.

"I'm sorry, sweetie," he said meekly. "This has gone too far."

Sweetie? Jackie-of-All-Trades and Doc Sherman weren't just coconspirators, they were a couple!

"What are you talking about, Sherm?" she snapped. "We've been over this already. We can't run away together and start a new life in the Caribbean without the gold, and we can't get the gold without getting rid of her."

"I want our dream life as much as you do, but it's not worth harming this young woman to get it. I should have put a stop to this as soon as Nancy wiped out on that ice instead of Chef K," he said. "I never should have let you talk me into putting her in that phony cast."

"The phony what?!" I exclaimed. "You mean my leg isn't really broken?"

Doc Sherman chewed his lip and looked down at the ground. "The small fracture of your ankle is real, but your hip is perfectly fine. I could have just put you in an ankle cast and a walking boot, but we knew you were a skilled detective, and Jackie wanted me to make sure you couldn't look too closely into what happened."

No wonder my hip hadn't hurt! And no wonder he'd been so insistent about confining me to bed rest! I realized then that the orders I'd heard Jackie giving someone over the walkie-talkie after the accident had been her instructing Doc Sherman to take me off the case before I realized there was one.

"We'd already faked one broken bone to give me my cover story," Jackie said. "It was easy enough to fake another to keep you from figuring it out."

"So I swapped the X-ray of your femur with another patient's, hoping a full leg cast would put you out of commission for the week," Doc Sherman explained.

"We hadn't planned on you cracking the case from a wheelchair."

"I told you we should have put her in a full-body cast," Jackie said bitterly.

"We would have had to send her out to the hospital, and they would have seen through the ruse in a second," he said. "I would have lost my license."

"You should lose your license!" I shot back. "Everything you've done is completely unethical!"

I was tempted to pull the fishing line and unleash the hot pepper on him, but acting out of anger wasn't going to get me anywhere. Doc Sherman's appearance may have helped me piece together their scheme, but now I was facing two bad guys instead of one. Or was I? I wasn't feeling optimistic enough to think the doc's regret made him my ally, but he definitely wasn't as committed to the plan.

"The ice trap that took you out may not have been meant for you, but we were still able to use it to our advantage, just like we can turn this situation to our advantage," Jackie said, then turned her glare on the doctor. "Now get over this guilt trip of yours, and help me get her into the secret passage before we get caught."

"And what do you plan to do with her once we take her there?" Doc Sherman asked.

"I hadn't gotten that far," Jackie admitted. "Things were moving too fast. We can figure it out later."

"Unless Nancy agrees to just forget about all this—" Doc Sherman began.

"Not likely," I interjected.

"Then we have to silence her," the doctor concluded ominously.

"Wait a second!" I objected. What happened to that other, nicer doc?

"Now you're talking, Sherm!" said Jackie. "Let's get to it!"

"I'm sorry, sweetie. I just can't do that. You have a concussion and you aren't thinking clearly," he said gently, assuming the kind, doctorly bedside manner that had been missing when he'd mistreated me in the clinic.

"I'm the *only one* thinking clearly," Jackie barked. "The way I see it, we can spend our retirement either living large on a tropical island or behind bars."

"That's a chance I'm willing to take," Doc said sadly. "It took you and Nancy almost being killed in that horrible snowmobile attack for me to realize it. That phony cast I put on Nancy put her life at risk, and our greed nearly cost me yours."

He walked over to Jackie and lovingly took her hand. "I can't bear the thought of you not being here anymore. And I can't bear to be the cause of any more misfortune. I took an oath to preserve life when I became a doctor. We got so caught up in chasing our dreams that we let it cloud our judgment. But we're good people, and I can't let a young woman come to more harm because of me. Sweetie, will you help me set this right?"

Jackie met Doc Sherman's pleading look. Then she lifted the ax.

"Fine, I'll do it myself," she said. "You'll thank me later when we're on the beach sipping banana daiquiris out of coconuts."

Jackie pulled her hand away from the doc and rushed toward me with the ax raised.

It suddenly dawned on me that if my ginormo cast was bogus and my femur wasn't really broken, then there was no reason for me to be confined to my chair. I pushed myself onto my feet, ignoring the pain in my ankle, and lunged clumsily for the buffet table by the window. It had been so long since I'd walked, my legs felt like Jell-O, but I didn't let that stop me from grabbing the coffee cup containing the leftover habanero powder.

"Jackie, no!" I heard Doc Sherman cry out behind me as her footsteps closed in.

I swung around, flinging the cup's contents at Jackie's face just before she reached me. She dropped the ax instantly and stumbled back, screaming.

Bull's-eye! The cupful of pepper powder hit her flush in the face!

But I didn't get to celebrate for long.

I backed up, trying to keep my balance as Jackie grabbed her face and started flailing around in a blind panic. First she careened into the table, sending a lamp crashing to the floor. Then she careened into me . . . knocking me right out of the open window!

CHAPTER TWENTY-THREE

Free Fall

GRAVITY INSTANTLY TOOK HOLD, PULLING me toward the ground two stories below. My body twisted in the air as I fell, and I somehow managed to grab hold of the window frame, first with one hand, then the other. My body slammed into the lodge's log exterior, but I managed to keep hold. Barely.

I tried to pull myself up, but the snow-covered frame's icy-cold exterior was too slippery. All I could do was hold on as tight as my frozen fingers let me and dangle. And look down. Big mistake! Vertigo made my head spin, and I nearly lost my grip.

A broken ankle was about to be the least of my worries if I fell. My only hope was that snow might break my fall enough that I didn't hurt myself *too* badly. One thing seemed certain—I was about to find out.

I looked up to see Doc Sherman appear in the window just as my fingers began to slip.

"Give me your hand!" he called, reaching down to grab me.

Jackie shoved him out of the way before he had a chance. Squinting at me through furious, painfully bloodshot eyes, she clawed at my hands, trying to pry up my fingers in one last desperate attempt to cover up her crimes.

The last thing I saw before I lost my grip and began to fall was Doc Sherman conking Jackie over the head with a candlestick.

And then I was falling. Freezing, snowy air rushed past me as I plummeted two stories toward the cold ground below. I shut my eyes, bracing myself for impact. The last thing I expected was to land in a fluffy fleece blanket.

When I opened my eyes, I saw two Christmas angels standing over me.

"Oh my God, Nancy, are you all right?" Liz asked.

"You're alive!" shouted Brady.

"Thanks to you guys I am—I think," I said in confusion, looking down at the cozy red blanket decorated in reindeer and candy canes I found myself lying on. "Did I really just fall out of a window, or am I dreaming?"

"We were taking a walk in the storm when we heard yelling coming from your room," Liz said in an excited rush. "Next thing we knew, you were falling from the sky!"

"Liz grabbed one of the blankets we used as a cape for the kids' snow vampires," Brady chimed in, pointing to a handful of snowmen with baby carrot fangs near the lodge's front door. All of them had blanket capes except one.

"We rushed over, held it up between us like one of those firemen's nets in the old cartoons, and hoped for the best," Liz said, looking me up and down with concern. "Are you sure you're okay?"

I took a quick inventory of my body. My ankle throbbed like crazy, which wasn't surprising, but so did my previously fine, fake-broken hip! "Ugh, I think I messed up my leg again. I don't think anything else is broken, though. I'm just a little more banged up than I already was."

"So, um, did we really just see Doc Sherman whack Jackie over the head with a candlestick?" Brady asked.

I looked back up at the empty window, the events of the last few minutes starting to come back to me in a jumbled rush after the shock of my fall.

"I think you did. We need to make sure Jackie doesn't go anywhere," I said. "But I'm pretty sure Doc is going to cooperate."

"You cracked the case?" Liz asked.

"Along with my leg, possibly," I said, wincing.

"You mean Jingly Jackie and the doc are the bad guys?" Brady asked in disbelief.

"Some of them," I said, my gut sinking as I looked down the hill, where the whine of chain saws carried up from somewhere inside the maze. "But right now the only bad guys I'm worried about are the ones down there."

"Nancy! Are you all right? What happened?" Archie yelled, running over to us with Henry and Carol right behind him, each of them wearing boots and jackets haphazardly thrown on over their pajamas. "Someone get the doctor!"

"He's up there," I said, looking up at the window I'd just fallen out of and then pointing down to the maze. "Don't worry about me—we need to help my friend Joe. The snowmobile thugs are chasing him through the maze!"

"Thugs in the maze? I don't understand." Archie looked down at me in bewilderment, along with the rest of the growing crowd of staff and guests who'd ventured outside to see what all the commotion was about. The lodge's backup generator must have kicked in, because lights started to come on all over the hotel, and I could see people pressed up against the glass in nearly all the occupied rooms too. And everyone was gawking down at me, the girl in the cast lying on a

Christmas blanket in the snow in the middle of a snowstorm. Everyone except for one person. The guy in the corner suite on the other end of the lodge.

Grant was looking out his window as well, only he was too busy watching the maze through his camera's telephoto lens to pay attention to the commotion going on right in front of the lodge.

There was only one reason why someone would be watching the darkened maze in the middle of a snowstorm: they knew what was going on inside it. Seeing him fixated on that instead of the girl who'd just fallen out of the window told me all I needed to know about the identity of Jackie's fall guy.

Jackie said the person she'd left the blackmail note for had something to hide, and I had a pretty good idea what it was.

Grant must have felt the psychic laser beams shooting from my eyes, because he finally turned away from the maze and looked down to see me pointing an accusing finger in his direction. He froze for a second, then dropped the camera and bolted from the window.

I didn't need my binoculars to know there was a look of pure panic on his face.

"Don't let Grant get away!" I shouted, wishing I could get up and give chase myself. "He's behind the snowmobile attacks!"

Liz and Brady ran inside after him, along with a couple of staff members.

"There must be some mistake," Archie said, looking crestfallen. "Grant wouldn't try to hurt anybody."

"I'm sorry, Archie, it's true," I told him. "He didn't have anything to do with the rest of the sabotage—that was Jackie and Doc Sherman—but Grant and whoever's been riding those snowmobiles are trying to cover up something big."

"There he is!" Carol yelled as Grant burst through one of the lodge's side doors and started trying to run for the parking lot. I don't know where he thought he was going in all that deep snow, but he didn't get far.

He'd made it only a few feet when he came face to rolling pin with Chef K. One blow from the heavy wooden kitchen implement and Grant was down for the count.

CHAPTER TWENTY-FOUR

The Twelve Suspects of Christmas

THAT WAS ONE MORE BAD GUY DOWN, BUT there were still two to go. Everyone was still gawking at Chef K standing over Grant with her rolling pin when Joe tumbled out of the maze and came running clumsily toward us as fast as the snow would let him.

"Help!" he screamed. "They have power tools!"

Everybody turned to look as the two enormous thugs burst through the maze after him, snow and

~ 325 ~

evergreen branches flying everywhere as they cut their way through the thick hedges with the chain saws.

They were dressed head to toe in white again, only this time one of them had lost his mask. When I'd seen their hulking silhouettes from afar, I'd thought it might be Dino Bosley and one of his buddies, or maybe even Sheriff Pruitt. Now that I could see a face, I knew I'd been wrong. It was still a face I recognized, though. I'd seen it on my ride past the protest in town on the way to the lodge that first day. On one of the enormous bodyguards escorting pipeline honcho Larry Thorwald out of the town hall. The same bodyguards Frank said had a reputation for beating up protesters. The ones Joe said were both nicknamed "Tiny." As soon as I saw the guy's face, I knew what Grant had written on the note Sheriff Pruitt took when he arrested Frank.

The two Tinys tore their way out of the maze, ready to pursue Joe with their chain saws, when they looked up to see a small crowd of shocked spectators gaping back at them—including the guy who had presumably called them, who was still lying in the snow

from Chef K's knockout blow. The Tinys put on t̶
brakes, turned to look at each other, then immediately
ran the other way.

Joe heard the chain saws go silent and cautiously
turned around to see his pursuers fleeing back through
the maze.

"Yeah, you better run!" he shouted after them.

Joe trudged up to us, panting, about the same time
Berkley arrived to give me my third rescue toboggan
ride of the week. I doubt anyone had ever gotten three
in one trip before! Grant got a toboggan too. Only his
was meant to keep him strapped down so he didn't
run away.

Archie stood over Grant's toboggan, looking
stricken, as the ski patrollers tightened the straps.

"I know whose number Grant wrote down on the
note after he got off the phone in the lounge," I said to
Joe. "It wasn't the initials *TS* for just one person, like
you guys thought. It stood for *T*s. As in capital *T* plu-
ral. As in *the T*s."

Joe winced as he unlocked the riddle for himself.

"The Tinys," he squeaked. "The phone number for Thorwald's bodyguards. Now you tell me!"

"Thorwald's bodyguards?" Archie asked, trying to make sense of the conversation.

"Yup, the scary, oversize, chain-saw-toting maniacs who just pruned your maze for you," Joe said.

Archie looked near tears as he stared down at his business partner. "Is this true, Grant?"

Grant had finally regained consciousness after Chef K knocked him out, and now he cracked under Archie's heartbroken glare.

"I'm sorry, Arch," he mumbled. "I didn't mean for anybody to get hurt, but Thorwald threatened to sic his goons on me instead if I didn't keep everything quiet. The Tinys were only supposed to scare Nancy off during the sleigh ride, not almost kill her!"

"What do you mean by 'everything'?" Archie asked hesitantly.

Grant clammed up again, so I filled Archie in instead. "That big stock purchase and the campaign contributions from the oil lobbyist weren't a coincidence or because of some campaign manager. Joe and Frank were right about Grant being entangled up to his eyeballs with the pipeline. So by 'everything' I think he basically means conspiring with Thorwald and his cronies to force the pipeline through and secretly get rich in the process."

"I think you left out lying to voters about his conflict of interest and violating public trust," Joe added.

"I'm guessing he was also leaking the truth about the resort's shaky finances to the pipeline people to help them force you into a deal," I told Archie reluctantly.

Archie stumbled back like he'd been hit. "How could you do this to me, Grant? To us! We shared this dream together! Grand Sky Lodge was supposed to show we could build a socially responsible, sustainable resort on our own terms without giving in to corporate greed or harming the planet!"

"I didn't mean to do anything wrong, Arch!" Grant said plaintively. "I just thought if I could get you to see how the lodge would benefit from leasing the land for the pipeline, it would be a win-win for everybody. It's just a tiny sliver of land, and we'd be able to pay all our loans, and you'd have plenty of extra money to use on more environmental projects. And it would help me politically. It's not like I meant to do anything illegal."

"You mean like insider trading?" Joe asked, cocking his eyebrow.

"Buying All Alloy's stock and lying to your business partner about it may not be illegal," I explained. "But buying it knowing you were secretly about to do something to personally drive up the price—"

"Like leasing a key piece of land to your buddy Thorwald's company so he could build an oil pipeline and buy lots of All Alloy parts," Joe clarified helpfully.

"That *is* illegal," I said.

Grant opened his mouth like he wanted to protest, but all that came out was, "Oh."

"And don't forget criminal conspiracy and accessory to every one of the ten or so violent crimes the Tinys committed trying to cover it up for you," I informed him.

"Things kind of spiraled out of control," Grant mumbled. "I was going to tell Thorwald I was done after what happened to Nancy on the sleigh, I swear, but . . ."

"But?" Archie demanded when Grant went silent again.

"Someone snuck back into my suite and left a blackmail note saying they knew what I'd done," Grant said, looking away in embarrassment. "And I panicked and called the Tinys to take care of it."

"Wait a second. We didn't leave the note in your suite!" said Joe.

"Oh that," I said, remembering I still hadn't gotten to fill Joe in on the full details of my run-in with Jackie before she tossed me out the window. "Jackie flipped the script on our script flip and left her own note for Grant, hoping he'd show up for the meet in the maze and we'd pin the sabotage on him instead—or he'd just have his friends take us out and save her the trouble."

"I didn't know it would be a teenager in the maze," Grant protested meekly.

"And that makes it any better?!" Archie yelled.

"My whole political career is at stake, Arch!" Grant whined.

"You're going to lose more than just your career, representative," I said. "You're going to lose your freedom."

Ski patrol dragged Grant off to the clinic to get checked out for a concussion and then lock him up somewhere safe until police could get there. Doc Sherman pushed my empty wheelchair out the hotel door a moment later, saying he had Jackie—who was going to need medical attention as well after getting conked on the head twice in one day—tied up in my suite and that he planned to cooperate fully.

"I'm sorry for the trouble I've caused everyone," he said, and chewed on his lip again. "If it's okay, I'd like to return to the clinic for now to treat everyone. I've caused enough harm, and it's about time I did something to help."

Archie looked to me.

"We can trust him," I said.

Archie nodded. "We should get you down to the clinic too, Nancy."

"No way," I said. "Not yet. It's possible that I broke my leg again, but I'm already in a full leg cast anyway.

I want some hot cocoa by the fireplace first."

"One hot cocoa coming up!" Henry said, marching back inside in his winter boots and jammies.

"Make that two hot cocoas, please," added Joe.

"With lots of marshmallows, please!" I called after him.

Soon I was nice and toasty and sipping hot cocoa by the lobby fireplace with Joe, watching the snow fall peacefully outside while we recapped the case.

"We've got Jackie and Doc Sherman cold on a treasure-hunting sabotage rap plus Grant for the pipeline conspiracy, along with plenty of evidence to send Tiny One, Tiny Two, and Thorwald down along with him," Joe said, taking a satisfied gulp of cocoa.

"Not bad for a night's work," I said, taking a satisfied gulp of my own.

"We sure have had a lot of suspects on this case," Joe commented.

"Clark, Marni, Carol, Dino, Sheriff Poo-it," I said, counting off the others.

"Don't forget Frank!" Joe said, laughing.

"Hey, it's like the twelve suspects of Christmas!" I said.

We both looked up as the grandfather clock across the lobby dinged midnight.

"Hey, do you know what that means?" I asked Joe, suddenly remembering this wasn't just any midnight. "It's officially Christmas Eve morning!"

"Merry Christmas, Drew," Joe said with a grin, raising his cup for a hot cocoa toast.

"Merry Christmas, Joe," I said, clinking cups. "There may not be any presents under the tree, but we sure did wrap up the bad guys!"

CHAPTER TWENTY-FIVE

All Wrapped Up

I WOKE UP THE NEXT MORNING TO sunshine and a brand-new full-leg cast, courtesy of a very apologetic Doc Sherman the night before. Liz and Brady's quick thinking may have broken my fall, but it didn't keep me from breaking my femur for real this time. Luckily—if you could call it that!—it was just a small fracture and I really would be in a walking boot soon.

A gift-wrapped leg wasn't exactly the present I was hoping for. Luckily—for real this time!—Archie had a surprise for me. First-class tickets for George,

Bess, and Ned to join me at the Grand Sky Lodge for Christmas! My dad, Hannah, and Fenton Hardy were joining us too!

The lodge would be closed for the holiday, so we'd have the whole place to ourselves. And Chef K was staying behind to celebrate with us and cook us our own private Christmas feast.

More holiday cheer followed in the form of a cleared, avalanche-free road and a state police caravan to drop Frank and Marni off and haul Grant, Jackie, and Doc Sherman away.

Dr. Sherman actually hugged me goodbye. I couldn't help feeling bad for him even after everything he had done. He'd been in love with Jackie for years, and she'd promised to leave her boyfriend and run away with him if he helped her find the gold. It looked like he was going to have a lot of time to think about what went wrong.

The Tinys were picked up by the state police after their snowmobiles ran out of gas on the highway out of town, and hopefully Thorwald was next—after the state's attorney got through his army of lawyers. Whether Thorwald was in custody or not, it definitely looked like the pipeline was kaput in Prospect, and maybe anywhere else for that matter.

This probably wasn't how they saw the trip with their high school environmental club going, but Frank and Joe came to Prospect to stop the pipeline, and with my help, they succeeded. Score a big one for the good guys!

Sheriff "Poo-it" Pruitt was suspended for misconduct with a full investigation pending, although so far it looked like the laws he'd broken didn't include being part of the pipeline conspiracy. He'd recognized the area code on the phone number Grant had written down just like the boys had, and he pocketed it and arrested Frank to protect his own self-interest in the pipeline and cover for Grant, not knowing exactly what he was covering for.

A very sleepy-eyed Carol had a surprise gift for me too: a preview of the feature she'd stayed up all night feverishly writing about how Nancy Drew and the

Hardy Boys saved the Grand Sky Lodge and stopped the pipeline! She didn't spare any of the unflattering sensational details, but she also gushed over the lodge's planet-friendly "eco-lux" amenities and Mountain to Table's fab food, so everyone came out looking great! Liz's nonprofit even got a shout-out!

A van arrived a few hours later with the new guests from River Heights. Bess fluttered her eyelashes and Joe melted. George ignored Frank and Frank melted. Ned kissed me on the cheek and I melted.

Now that the whole team was together, we had one last unsolved mystery to crack.

CHAPTER TWENTY-SIX

And to All a Good Night

THE SIX OF US ENTERED THE SECRET chamber turned food pantry under the restaurant armed with the torn parchment treasure map Dr. Sherman had given us. With the blessing of a kinder, gentler, very grateful Chef K, my friends carefully removed all the food from the north wall and disassembled her new custom shelves to reveal the long-hidden door concealed behind them.

The cobweb-filled tunnel was just wide enough to fit my wheelchair. At first it seemed like nobody had been inside the dusty tunnel in over a hundred years, but the recent footprints in the earthen floor said differently. We didn't have to follow the trail of footprints far before we saw the old wooden chest.

The treasure was real! And poor Jackie had been only steps away from finding it before Chef K unwittingly cut her search short by closing off her kitchen to outsiders.

Everyone gathered around me as I slowly lifted the lid and shone my flashlight inside. A flash of gold sparkled from within, and we all gasped at once. But it wasn't because of the size of the treasure. Inside the nearly empty ancient chest, a single small gold nugget had been left as a paperweight, holding down a note written on Grand Sky Lodge stationery.

I pulled out the handwritten note and read it aloud:

> *Dear Jackie,*
> *Turns out you're not the only one who*
> *is good at snooping on people behind*
> *their backs. Thanks for leading me to the*
> *treasure! Didn't know I was watching,*

did you? Look us up if you ever make it to
the Caribbean.

Your newly retired (and filthy rich
thanks to you!) ex-boss,
Mrs. Bos

I thought about the portrait in the lobby of kooky ex-owner Mrs. Bosley in her Hawaiian shirt and smiled. It looked like she'd found her family's legendary lost gold and struck it rich at the Grand Sky Lodge after all.

Dear Diary,

THIS IS ONE HOLIDAY SEASON I WON'T soon forget. I can't believe all the false leads there were in this case. And multiple culprits with totally different motives! It's enough to make anyone's head spin. I have to admit, it was nice to have help from the Hardy Boys. I can't believe I once saw them as rivals! Turns out this resort was big enough for *three* teenage detectives.

Celebrate ninety years of
NANCY DREW
with this specially redesigned collection
of the first ten Nancy Drew Diaries!